Text Classics

OLGA MASTERS was born in Pambula, on the far south coast of New South Wales, in 1919. Her first job, at seventeen, was at a local newspaper, where the editor encouraged her writing. She married at twenty-one and had seven children, working part-time as a journalist for papers such as the *Sydney Morning Herald*, leaving her little opportunity to develop her interest in writing fiction until she was in her fifties.

In the 1970s Masters wrote a radio play and a stage play, and between 1977 and 1981 she won a series of prizes for her short stories. Her debut collection, *The Home Girls*, won a National Book Council Award in 1983. It was followed by a novel, *Loving Daughters*, which was highly commended for the same award. Her next books, the linked stories *A Long Time Dying* and the novel *Amy's Children*, met with critical acclaim. This brief but highly prolific period ended when Masters died, following a short illness, in 1986. She had been at work on *The Rose Fancier*, a posthumously published collection of stories.

Reporting Home, a selection of Masters' extensive journalism, was published in 1990. A street in Canberra bears her name.

EVA HORNUNG lives in South Australia. Writing as Eva Sallis, she won the *Australian*/Vogel and Dobbie awards her first novel, *Hiam*. *Mahjar* won the Steele Rudd Award and *The Marsh Birds* won the Asher Literary Award. Her most recent novel, *Dog Boy*, won the Prime Minister's Literary Award for fiction and, in Sweden, the Stora Ljudbokspriset.

ALSO BY OLGA MASTERS

The Home Girls (stories)
Loving Daughters
A Long Time Dying (stories)
Amy's Children
The Rose Fancier (stories)

Non-fiction
Reporting Home (ed. Deirdre Coleman)

Amy's Children
Olga Masters

Text Publishing Melbourne Australia

textclassics.com.au
textpublishing.com.au

The Text Publishing Company
Swann House
22 William Street
Melbourne Victoria 3000
Australia

First published by University of Queensland Press 1987
This edition published by The Text Publishing Company 2013

Cover design by WH Chong
Page design by Text
Typeset by Midland Typesetters

Printed in Australia by Griffin Press, an Accredited ISO AS/NZS 14001:2004
Environmental Management System printer

Primary print ISBN: 9781922147080
Ebook ISBN: 9781922148162
Author: Masters, Olga, 1919–1986.
Title: Amy's children / by Olga Masters; introduced by Eva Hornung.
Series: Text classics.
Dewey Number: A823.3

This book is printed on paper certified against the Forest Stewardship
Council® Standards. Griffin Press holds FSC chain-of-custody
certification SGS-COC-005088. FSC promotes environmentally
responsible, socially beneficial and economically viable management
of the world's forests.

CONTENTS

The Drifter
by Eva Hornung

OLGA Masters believed in the innate goodness of people. Yet her clear-eyed engagement with the failings, mistakes and harm that we do is a touchstone of her writing. Goodness, for Masters, is not a trite or universally shared concept. It has great breadth. To be human is to be good; and to be human is also to be limited, and to do harm to oneself and others. This fraught and tormented goodness underlies her crueller sketches as much as it does her richly developed main characters.

Masters explores in her fiction the lives of the women she observed around her. These women—children, teenagers, mothers, daughters, sisters, spinsters—are the core of her work, more so than her fine portraits of fathers, brothers, sons and lovers. Throughout her novels and stories we sense a keen interest in the lives of ordinary people. Much irony in her writing derives from the interplay between the mores and expectations that hem us in, and our inevitable amoral striving for self-fulfilment. She understood the effect of intellectual poverty in blinding young women to themselves and their world, and late in her life she observed with wry humour:

> Not only were we naïve by today's standards, but downright ignorant. Jogging was something we did when the butcher was selling sausages without asking for meat coupons. Heroin would have sounded like the name of a bird. We never knew of a child dying of cancer. The pill was taken for constipation. Gay was the way we felt most of the time, even while twenty-two thousand Australian men and women were prisoners of the Japanese.

As an ignorant young woman myself, I absorbed the news of Olga Masters' death in 1986 through the gossip of academic corridors. I had no idea she was sixty-seven. I thought of her as a young woman my age, with my own aspirations and literary ambitions, and I avoided reading her. What delight was mine when I finally discovered *The Home Girls*, *A Long Time Dying*, *Loving Daughters* and *Amy's Children*.

Masters wrote later in life, after raising seven children. She worked as a journalist from the age of fifteen and went on to write a column for the *Sydney Morning Herald*. In 1982 she published her first book, the short-story collection *The Home Girls* (it too is now a Text Classic), having won several awards for her stories. *Amy's Children* was published in 1987, not long after Masters' death from cancer.

She did not publish many works, but in a sense they were a lifetime in the making. Her son the renowned journalist Chris Masters has said that Masters' career began 'not when her first book was published, but when she started taking an interest in her neighbours'. He describes growing up 'in a house full of words', serving, with his brothers and sisters, 'an apprenticeship in storytelling'.

In his words, Olga Masters had the 'ability to get people to talk', a 'genuine curiosity'. Her style, sharp and translucent to great depths, offers us a fresh, sometimes startling understanding of everyday lives. She is as crisp and deft in dealing with child-hatred, incestuous desires, violence and our most suppressed motivations as with sibling rivalry, envy and love. This is part of the charm of these books.

Amy's Children is, in my view, the finest of them: polished, subtle and sustained, a rich portrait of inner-Sydney life. This classic Australian novel gives unique insight into wartime Australia, a period that is now the stuff of national myth and legend. However, *Amy's Children* is not merely about that time, or any time: as with all enduring works, it has the specific tactile connection with its world that makes the past live on in the present.

The novel is light and spiky; witty, wry and compassionate. We experience the small lives of its characters without judgement, yet with a keen awareness of how repelled we might have been by them had the book invited us to activate rather than circumvent our prejudices. Amy herself does much for which she would have been condemned, then and now. At the beginning of the story she leaves for the big city, abandoning her three children, which the title highlights as the action that defines the book.

She denies her eldest, Kathleen, a parental relationship; resents the intrusion of her children's needs and demands on her independent life; rejects and is rejected by her youngest daughter; and then embraces in hope and mysterious maternal feelings an impending arrival. All along, Amy, with an innocent animal selfishness, struggles for tiny and heartfelt material joys, little achievements in independence or lifestyle. Times are hard, and just making do is fraught with pitfalls. There is no room for the children she had while still barely out of childhood herself.

'Whatever's that?' Daphne cried, coming down the hall. The little drawers answered her, running eagerly out and back as Peter tipped them. He laughed and set the chest down and stood back to admire it.

'Was it alright to buy it, Aunty Daph?' Amy asked, pleased with their faces.

In her bedroom Amy set it against the wall opposite the foot of her bed. Admiring it she backed until she sat on the bed.

Daphne was in the doorway. 'More for a little girl's room. But lovely.'

Amy was about to tip the contents of her suitcase, in which she stored her underwear, onto her bed to transfer them to the drawers. Instead she went with bowed head and put her fingers into the open parts of the plaited cane that made a frame for the mirror. They did not easily fit but the fingers of Kathleen and Patricia would have. She turned away and smoothed the bed where she sat. Someday I'll have them with me, she thought, and it's a good idea to start getting some things together.

Amy abandons her children, yet genuinely loves them, intermittently. She holds us—holds our empathy—regardless. Despite all her attempts to find firm footing and the furniture of a secure life, she drifts at the mercy of her circumstances, subject to the whims and pressures of her employer, her eldest daughter, her aunt, her two dreadful lodgers, and most of all her emotions and slowly maturing womanhood.

This drifting quality in Amy's motivations is for me the novel's most poignant element. She falls in love with her cousin; she finds her oily boss repellent, but ends up attracted to him. Her three daughters barely register in her thoughts, except as guilt, until they present themselves and make demands. Her life is precarious, derailed by the slightest pressure one way or another, at the mercy of her own inchoate feelings; yet she holds herself with a hope and naïve pride that make her compelling.

And we know, at the end of the book, that her struggle will continue. Kathleen's blind anger and disgust, infused with her own unique arrogance and self-interest, leaves them both vulnerable. Amy's choices are curtailed, and her only assistance will again be her hard-bitten family. At the same time, we believe in Amy's instinctive strength. The conclusion, in which she defines her relationship with each of her offspring, is moving and deeply ironic.

Amy is a wonderfully drawn character: someone who is, in the most complex sense, innately good; someone in whom we recognise our own unacknowledged fickle, driven selves. It is about time we had her back.

Amy's Children

For my children

1

Ted Fowler left his wife Amy and the children when the youngest, another girl, was a few weeks old.

The infant was sickly. The Great Depression was in a much more robust state. Ted told Amy he was going to walk south to Eden where there was reported to be work on fishing boats.

Ted and Amy had been married for only three years.

The first child was born three months after the wedding. Eighteen months later there was another and fifteen months after that a third.

Amy's parents, Gus and May Scrivener, and her brothers Norman and Fred lived on their farm a couple of miles outside Diggers Creek where Ted and Amy had their first and only home.

Amy got herself with child at seventeen.

May's anger, disgust and disappointment were tempered just slightly by her liking for Ted. He had a way with his eyes of making May feel more Amy's age than her own, showing a willingness to fetch and carry for her at dances and cricket matches and picnics, most of which she organized.

Whether officially in charge or not, May tended to take the lead, impatient with those of lesser energy, and this, aided by the sharpness of her tongue, earned her a reputation for bossiness.

Diggers Creek, on the outskirts of the little town of Tilba Tilba, was a hamlet of school, post office, public hall, general store and All Souls Anglican Church.

Not all the Anglican souls of Diggers Creek attended the services conducted by a visiting minister from Tilba Tilba.

Sometimes all the pews were empty, and when this happened the sermons and the hymns were of necessity bypassed, and the minister said a few prayers, his eyes on the starlings' nests in the rafters above the altar. He was not discouraged by the sight, for the gaps letting in the birds grew wider each time he came to Diggers Creek. The time should not be too far off when the roof would cave in and there would be an end to the fruitless visits there.

But the church came to life (the starlings' nests swept ruthlessly away by May's broom) for Amy's wedding.

May and Amy went to Tilba Tilba to make the necessary arrangements. They talked with the minister around Amy's swollen belly, Amy believing her condition was not obvious to him and May half believing it too.

4

"A very nice man," she said on the way home, indulging in a little dream that Amy married him, not Ted, in a bizarre turn of events in which Ted died suddenly (though painlessly), and Amy gained respectability which sealed forever the gossiping lips of Diggers Creek.

But the minister lost ground when the marriage ceremony was over and he told Amy and Ted he expected them back in the church for the child's christening.

"It was his job to do the joinin' and he was paid for that!" May said at the house afterwards. (She had paid the ten shillings marriage fee without Gus knowing.)

Everyone at the wedding breakfast was impressed by her optimism and good spirits. With an apron over her brown crepe dress, she was setting food out on a long table on the back veranda shaded by a grapevine.

For Ted was out of work and Gus not speaking to him or Amy. He refused to go to the wedding and was now digging a new garden by the back fence, visible to the wedding guests through the grapevines. The round country faces expressed neither concern nor surprise at the spectacle of the spade flashing silver when it parted from the black earth, and Gus's old working coat flying halfway up his back with his constant bending and straightening.

May's words brought a degree of comfort to the wedding guests. Many, though of Anglican faith, went to church only for weddings and funerals, and were pleased to hear a dark side of the minister's character exposed. They could now dismiss any feelings of guilt occasioned by their wayward habits and get on with the fun of the breakfast.

"The joinin' had been well and truly done, anyway," one whispered to another, sneaking a look at Amy's belly from a fresh angle.

May's mood changed when the guests were gone. She was left with the cleaning up, for Amy went immediately to her bedroom, throwing off her wedding dress and following it with her pants, since Ted came in after her and shut the door.

May went into a fury of rattling plates and cups and flinging off the cloth from the table, dodging about, using her knees to send the chairs skittering across the boards, half encouraged, half infuriated at the sight of Gus outside, spading with an energy threatening to outstrip hers.

"Everything left to me!" she cried aloud, feeling an urge to break the quiet of the house, for the boys had gone to bring in the cows for the afternoon milking.

"No movement from in there!" She raised the broom she had seized and aimed it like a gun at the front of the house where Ted and Amy were. "Bang, bang, bang! Then sleep it off. Bang, bang, bang! There we go for a dozen more!"

She flung the broom away at last, like a child worn out with temper, abandoning all hope of attention, and went and sat by the kitchen door to watch Gus, who seemed shrunken now beside the great mound of weeds and grass and bruised and tangled vines.

"Well he might!" May said. "There'll be extra mouths to fill and if it doesn't come from the ground or out of a tree, there's nowhere else and nothing else but to go hungry!"

Her eye caught the leftover food from the wedding feast—a ruin of corned beef, firm in the centre, the outside

6

shredded, as if it had been cooked with a ball of string, and half a very yellow cake, iced in strong pink. A pile of rock cakes was pressed against the cut side of the cake.

The Scriveners would have that for tea. The food and the cleaned-up kitchen and veranda pleased May, and her expression had softened by the time Ted came from the bedroom, trying to look innocent of the act of removing his clothes and putting them on again. May ran her eyes over him and Ted's eyes followed for a check on buttons.

"Not too much of that from now on," May said. "It could bring on a miscarriage." Even Ted nearly smiled, since a miscarriage was what they had hoped for. And May snapped the door shut on the dresser and her secret dream for a natural end to the pregnancy.

She had thought the wedding a big enough hurdle to overcome.

"We'll get this over and done with first," she said to anyone within earshot. Now there were hurdles, she could see, of even greater height. Ted was without regular work, there was no money for furniture if they found a place to rent, and Gus was intolerant of having them under his roof.

She tucked a chair smartly under the table, resisting an impulse to sit, surprising Ted who was expecting an extension of the homily on restricting intercourse (which he would not do whatever she said).

She charged down to join Gus, who had by this time dug a width of earth like a giant chocolate bar by the back paling fence. There was little else to the Scriveners' backyard—a few ragged rosebushes with tough whitish coloured grass wrapped around the roots, a scarred and thorny lemon tree and a peach, the trunk grey and scaly like the skin of an alligator.

May stooped and shook dirt from the grass as the sods left Gus's spade. She was there to berate him, but the earth in her hands was soothing. The thought of the new vegetable crop was soothing too, and its nearness to the kitchen, for their pumpkins and beans were normally grown between the furrows in the corn paddock. But Gus's digging had been inspired solely by his contempt for the wedding, and she was not ready to offer outright forgiveness.

"You humiliated me as usual," she told him, taking a rake to drag together some heaps of grass and weeds. "A wedding for your own daughter and you don't come near it!"

Gus decided to stop for a smoke now that work was in progress without him. He took his tobacco from a rail of the fence, and with his legs apart and his head down he stuck a paper to his bottom lip and rubbed the tobacco in the palm of his hand. He was pleased with his digging, getting a good look at it for the first time. His face took on a contented look as if everything else had been placed on a closed shelf of his mind, and the new garden was all that mattered.

May began to stroke the ground clean of the weeds left behind in the first rake. The short grass was like hair being combed, the ground seemed to purr under the strokes, fine strands clinging to the teeth of the rake as hair does to a comb.

"Roll yourself one," Gus said, handing May his tobacco. He sniffed with a cocked nose towards the house. "You'd need something calmin' after that rort."

May sat on the ground, lifting her knees, her dress over them in tent fashion.

She watched the shreds of yellow-green tobacco turn into a little golden-brown mould, tipping it then onto the paper. Everything connected with rolling a smoke was a joy—pinching out the stray ends of tobacco from the tight little roll, wetting the one end, then lighting the other just on the tip, a perfect light, not blazing halfway down the paper, not even scorching it, a sensuous feeling holding it between two fingers, then taking the first draught of smoke, all but peace leaving her mind as the smoke left her mouth, moving sensuously too, putting a frail screen between her and Gus.

Ted crossed the veranda, jumping to the ground without using the steps, and walked jauntily up to them. "Hullo, Mum and Dad!"

"Pass me back that tobacco, May," Gus said.

2

Amy and the children moved in with Gus and May when Ted left.

There was hardly any furniture for Amy to worry about. Food and rent for their small grey house next to the Diggers Creek Post Office accounted for the little Ted earned when he got a few months' work with a road gang after Kathleen was born. Patricia came next and then the baby Lesley.

May said it might have been different, Ted might have stayed if the child had been a boy, and Amy, blaming herself, did the best she could and gave her the male-sounding name of Lesley.

Amy sat a lot of the time on the edge of the veranda, nursing the restless whimpering infant and looking out for Ted to return.

One day she went inside, trailed by Kathleen and Patricia, and still with the baby in her arms, pushed the furniture together for Norman or Fred to come and collect it in the farm truck and return it to the Scriveners, for the stretcher beds, food safe, table and two chairs had been roped for a dozen years to the rafters of the corn shed. They were discarded from the farmhouse to make room for furniture inherited when May's parents died and their possessions were divided between May and her sister Daphne.

Amy put the yelling baby on one of the stretchers while she rolled up the mattress on the other, the blankets and sheets inside. She then told Kathleen to sit on the floor with her legs stretched out, and laid the baby across them while she did the same with the other bed. The baby yelled on while she packed her one tablecloth and few face and tea-towels among the groceries in the food safe, and bound a piece of rope around the safe to stop the door flying open.

She put the kettle, two saucepans, a frying pan and a tea caddy in an old butter box. The box was one Kathleen and Patricia pushed around the floor pretending it was a dolls' pram. Sometimes it was a car or train carriage pulled by a rope bound to two nails Amy hammered in the corners where the wood joined.

Kathleen's eyes widened and her face paled at this misuse of her plaything. But any protest would have been drowned by the screams of the baby. So she pressed her lips together and relieved her feelings with a wild rocking of her body, hoping this might quieten the child as well. But Lesley screamed on, with a vein throbbing alarmingly in her thin little neck.

Amy hoisted the two old suitcases that held their clothing onto the table and packed a billycan with wrung-out wet

11

napkins for Kathleen to carry. After she'd put some clean napkins in an old leather bag she flung over her shoulder, she took the baby and they were ready to go.

She had no free hand so she closed the front door with her foot. Kathleen gave her free hand to Patricia and turned her sturdy little body around when they were on the road to look back on the house, pretty sure she was not going to live there any more.

The legs of the little girls miraculously held out until the last half mile, when Kathleen had to take both basket and billycan and Amy had to take Patricia on her hip.

Gus and May were in amiable conversation over the dinner table when they walked in. It was clear to them what had happened, and Kathleen made it clearer by hooking the handle of the billycan over the tap, as had been the practice at their place.

"Take those dirty things to the wash house," May said quite sharply. "They'll bring flies just when I got the place clear of them."

She rose and began to clear the table, taking a pile of plates to dump in the washing-up dish, then dumping the dish on a corner of the table. She saw Amy looking hardly older than Kathleen, with Patricia crushed to her side on the couch and the baby on its stomach, sleeping across her lap as if it had undertaken the long walk and was more worn out than the others. Patricia's eyes were round and scared, and looking from them to Amy's, May saw hardly any difference at all.

She slapped crumbs from the breadboard, slapped the blade of the knife on the tablecloth to clean it, and seizing a loaf began to saw slices off.

Kathleen put her chin on the table. "Oh, good!" she said.

"Look out or you'll get cut!" said May.

Gus left his chair and went out.

Amy gave May her only income, the Child Endowment paid by the Government for children other than the eldest. The Government's theory was that parents, however feckless, should be able to provide for an only offspring, the offer of payments for more being an incentive to have them, despite the hard times.

She would dream of having a job, buying a new dress and silk stockings and a blue band for her hair to go to the Tilba Tilba dances.

She sometimes dreamed aloud on the front veranda, sitting between Kathleen and Patricia, with her feet among the arum lilies growing thickly on either side of the front steps.

"Mummy might get a job one day, you never know," she said once, her eyes on a car racing along the road, going south. It might stop, she said silently, a man might get out and come up to me and say, I've got a job for you in my big shop. There will be clothes for you very cheap, and clothes for the girls. Come on, I'll give you half an hour to get ready. All she needed to do was to wipe their faces and go.

She looked from one to the other and buttoned the back of Patricia's dress and pinched it straight on the shoulders, the child's eyes asking questions. Kathleen brushed some dirt from her legs and pulled her skirt down. They had no shoes on, but there would not be a long wait for new ones.

The car had gone but there was another coming. Perhaps this time, Amy thought. The baby cried and Kathleen took a sharp breath and watched Amy's face.

"Lebby's crying," she said gently as if Amy were sleepwalking and she didn't want to shock her into waking. In a moment there were footsteps inside and the crying stopped. "Granma's got her," Kathleen said.

Inside herself Amy said, I won't be taking her.

3

She didn't either. Or for that matter the other two.

When Lesley was a few months old Amy got work in Moruya at one of the hotels. It took days of grumbling from May to agree to her going, for she could not take the children and could see them only on her days off. The visits would be infrequent since Amy would have to get a lift with someone travelling Diggers Creek way. There would be problems getting back to the hotel. And taking the mail car on its way through Moruya to Diggers Creek meant arriving at Scriveners late in the afternoon and an overnight stay to catch the car early the next morning. Only one full day at a time was given staff so Amy would need to make arrangements with the management (a weak little man and his overpowering wife) to take the mail car, and the cost would take nearly all her weekly wage.

Only once did Amy come home this way. Mrs Turner was away in Melbourne on a week's holiday, and Mr Turner, who admired Amy's round little bottom and the way her smile went right back to the last of her teeth, told her to go off and see her children, and gave her five shillings from the bar till, slamming it shut straight away, as if he was afraid of changing his mind, or Mrs Turner was able to hear although she was several hundred miles away.

Amy sat on the couch for the first hour of her visit and nursed Patricia with Kathleen pressed to her side. May walked about getting things done in the kitchen with Lebby on one hip. Amy didn't see much of the baby's face for she had her forehead pressed to May's shoulder, a few curls parted to show a tender, creamy neck.

Amy called out "Lesley!" and stretched out an arm. "Here's Mum!" she said, only feebly pleading.

The baby pressed harder into May.

"We call her Lebby all the time," Kathleen said.

"She's not shy all the time," Patricia said, gently cruel.

Kathleen felt the stuff of Amy's dress, blue with a diamond pattern of a deeper blue linked by narrow swirls.

"Mumma's dress has diamonds and ribbons on it," Kathleen said.

May moved Lebby to her other shoulder.

"Not too many diamonds and ribbons around this place," she said, laying a cooking spoon on a saucer.

Amy loosened the arm around Patricia, and taking her handbag from behind her took out a ten shilling note. She had to stretch across the children to lay it on the end of the table. Kathleen expected May to reach down from her end

16

and snatch it up, but it appeared she had no interest in it at all, which seemed strange, for May was always expressing a wish for more money, and she would look through the mail when Kathleen brought it from the box at the gate, anxious for something from Amy and wearing a closed dark face when there were only catalogues and bills.

The money looked as if it might blow off the table, lying there by a fork at her grandfather's place. Kathleen rushed forward and slid it under the fork. May, terrified her eyes might be forced to meet Amy's, swooped on the fork, disturbing Lebby, and pushed the note off with the prongs. It fluttered to the floor and Kathleen turned scandalized eyes to her mother.

"Leave it stay there," May said. She dragged Lebby's high chair to the table and sat her there, the child screwing herself around until her back was to Amy, again showing the little piece of neck. Kathleen went to her side and patted the hands gripping the chair arm. Amy went to the bedroom and came back in a black dress she wore to wait on tables at the hotel.

Lebby screamed and flung herself on Kathleen with such force the chair tipped and Kathleen had to fling herself on Lebby to right it.

"It's that black dress," May shouted, taking the warmed plates from the back of the stove. "She saw a nun once in Tilba and cried for a week afterwards."

She set down the roast of beef which looked like a small grey hut with a yellow roof, then took Lebby out of her chair and sat with her on a rocker. Kathleen went and sat by her mother. She always loved to see May rocking

Lebby, but now she hated the grinding of the rockers on the hearth and imagined Amy winced, as if they were grinding into her flesh.

Kathleen slipped a hand under Amy's arm, soft like her own, and tried to gauge by the feel if Amy was terribly hurt by Lebby's rejection of her.

Gus came in for dinner and saw the note and picked it up. Bloody silly women, said the disgusted look he flicked from face to face. He pinned the money under a milk jug.

"Take her," May said to Gus and left the rocker. Gus sat and Lebby pressed herself against his rough old coat. He rubbed his bristly cheeks, first one and then the other, on the top of Lebby's head. Lebby's lips began to lift at the corners then stretch out. Mumma will see her new teeth, Kathleen thought, watching. Patricia left the couch and laid her body across Gus's knees face downwards. Gus parted his legs so that she almost fell through, righting his legs in time to save her. She laughed and Lebby did too. Gus carried on the game of widening his legs when it was least expected he would, then clamping them together unexpectedly too. Above the beef she was slicing, May's face softened with a quirking of her lips. Kathleen tried not to smile but couldn't help herself.

This is the last time I'll come home, Amy thought.

4

She did come home again when Lebby was nearly two and as shy as ever.

That's good, Amy thought, looking briefly at the legs dangling from May's hip, deceptively frail, she thought, wondering if she should carry the memory away with her.

She had saved her fare on the mail car to Nowra and there was enough left for a rail ticket to Sydney and a few pounds in case she did not get work straight away. She would stay with her Aunt Daphne in Annandale. May and her sister corresponded fairly regularly. "You know the address if you feel like a look at the Big Smoke," Daphne said in one of her letters. But Amy decided not to write and warn Daphne of her impending arrival. It might set up a conspiracy between her and May to prevent Amy getting away. It might be hard to convince Daphne from a distance of her intention of ultimately setting up house for herself and the children.

She had made up her mind to have nothing stand in her way. People staying at the hotel said Sydney was the place to be.

Once on her afternoon off she had put on her blue dress and sat on the veranda with a traveller in soft goods taking a seat beside her. He had a wife Elsie and two young children living at Bondi. He told Amy they had only to walk along the tram route past a few shops and there was the sea. Amy saw it rolling in blue as the last rinse on wash day, and the sand fawn coloured like the inside of a shell. Amy thought immediately of Lebby's neck but dismissed it.

She waited in the hope that the man would say to come and stay with them (if she was not welcomed at Daphne's) until she found somewhere permanent to live. But he smiled at his joined hands in his lap and she suspected he was thinking of the cosiness of his little home. So he was. "You should visit us in Sydney if you come," he said. "Elsie would make you very welcome."

In bed that night she imagined the sea washing onto the beach with a sleepy laziness, not crashing in cruelly as it had done once when Gus and May took her and the boys to the coast for a picnic when she was ten. She had whimpered in her wet cold state and Gus had been disgusted at her screams when he held her above a wave and let it slosh over her feet. He had all but thrown her back to May and the picnic basket, having made great sacrifices, working nearly all night to get their old truck going to get them there.

But the sea at Bondi would be different. The big waves too far out to be a worry, so gentle when they rolled onto the beach she could lie and let them wash over her. She went on to dream of a bathing suit, red perhaps, cut low on her back, which would be tanned a deep honey colour.

Gus left the kitchen when Amy announced her plans. "Gus!" May called, but he was gone.

May was ironing and she put such urgency into her work all of sudden, Kathleen on the floor with her rag doll connected the ironing with the going away. She had a vision of Amy walking along the road with a great heap of ironed clothes balanced on her arm. She blushed at the foolishness of this when she saw there were many of Gus's and the boys' things in the pile, and changed the vision to all of them walking, spread out from one side of the road to the other. Tears came into her eyes at the thought that she might not be carried when her legs grew tired because Patricia and Lebby would be taken up first. She pressed herself against her mother to communicate this fear to her and seek reassurance through the warm flesh of Amy's side.

Amy, seeking reassurance herself, clung to Kathleen and Patricia, one on either side of her, and looked at her big case, dropped inside the kitchen door, to gain comfort from that. It was packed with almost everything she owned and she planned not to unpack most of it since she would leave for Sydney in two days' time.

She watched May toss each ironed garment onto the pile. Lebby, in her chair at the corner of the table, bent towards May, eyes lowered. May murmured small soothing words every now and again.

"I'll get myself a better job there," Amy pleaded, and loosened her hold on the girls to slide her hands over her knees and look at them, telling herself they were capable of better things than making beds and sweeping floors.

Kathleen pressed harder against her, feeling the change in Amy's body as if it had been a warm and friendly tree trunk until she spoke. Now it was cold, and she felt that she was out in the paddocks alone with a storm coming and that the tree, afraid for itself, was no longer concerned with sheltering her. She picked up her doll from the floor and wrapped her arms around it. Amy stood up and with a little frown inspected some wrinkles on her sleeves and concentrated for a moment on stroking them away.

May gave her one brief, sharp look, ironing on with her free hand on Lebby's shoulder. The look said Damn your dress! Is that all you care about? Amy picked up her case and all eyes, even Lebby's, watched her as she carried it into the bedroom.

May finished the ironing. Kathleen was surprised to see the basket empty. Nearly always there was something left in the bottom, some of the boys' old shirts, too tattered to stand up to the rigours of May's thrusting iron. Emptiness took hold of her too. Something is changing, she thought, seeing the late afternoon sun had moved to the edge of the veranda boards and was clinging there, growing paler as she watched. That chilled her too, and she didn't know where to look for comfort.

Then May called from the end of the table, where she was rolling the ironing blanket into a fat little log, with the scorched part of the sheet hanging some tattered tongues out one end.

"Feed the fowls, Kathleen. Any minute they'll start up a squawk to deafen us all!"

Bent low like a runner starting a big race, Kathleen flew to the end of the veranda to scoop a jam tin of corn from an open bag there. She had to grapple with the legs of a chair to get to the corn, for the boys had thrown Amy's furniture there when they brought it from her place, and were paying no heed to May's constant pleas to take it to the shed where it belonged.

Kathleen ran with the corn to fling it over the wire netting into the pens. Setting up a squawking and fluttering of wings, the fowls threw themselves against the wire, scrambling on each other's backs and pecking at the air.

"Stop your noise!" she said, throwing the corn over their backs to the far side of the pen, causing them to turn and run in that direction, gobbling wildly under the shower of grain.

The mass of backs, Kathleen thought, looked like the grey patterned eiderdown on her grandmother's bed.

"Eat and be quiet!" she called. "Or my granma will be very angry with you!"

Running back with the empty tin she saw May hook her hair behind her ear in the old way, setting the table for tea.

We're not going, no one's going, we're not going, I know we're not going, she sang inside her head.

5

The getting away was terrible.

Kathleen was very white and Patricia buried herself in the corner of the couch and cried quietly like a grown-up. Lebby had a fever and May had put her into the double bed under the speckled eiderdown. It was ironic that May should spare Lebby from witnessing the departure, since she was the one least troubled by it.

When Amy came into the kitchen with her luggage, Patricia made for the corner of the couch and Kathleen ran to Gus and clung to his leg. He lifted her up, with a brief look of hate towards Amy, across Kathleen's tangled head for it was quite early in the morning, and May had not found time so far to comb Kathleen's and Patricia's hair and wipe their faces with a damp cloth. Kathleen thought how strange it was to see Amy dressed up with a hat on at that hour and a thick coating of lipstick. Beside her the kitchen seemed in even worse confusion. The teacups from the first pot, made when the boys and Gus had got up for the milking, waited beside the stack of porridge plates and rounds of bread, ready for what the farming community called second breakfast, taken in more leisurely fashion when the chores were done.

Amy took a piece of bread and ate it dry, pushing it through her red lips, eyes very round.

"If Fred is finished I'll get him to carry my port down," Amy said, laying the bread on the tablecloth.

"Come on," Gus said to Kathleen and hitched her higher, to carry her nearly at a run towards the dairy.

May scooped Patricia up and ran after them. "We'll see the poddies fed!" she cried.

Amy set off for the gate, bent sideways with the weight of her case. Fred saw, and ran to catch her up and take it, while she ran ahead to stop the car, wobbling down the rough track on her high heels. The car made a great deal of dust stopping suddenly. Climbing in, Amy got a showering on her navy skirt. Since she had not said any formal goodbyes to the others, she was too embarrassed to say goodbye to Fred and fussed with her handbag, looking inside it and snapping it shut and slapping at some imaginary dust on it. Only once did she lift her head to see Fred's round hungry face under his round felt hat, and beyond him Patricia running screaming towards the road (she couldn't hear the screaming but she saw it)—and Kathleen standing stiff like a small stone statue, and May with her fist raised shaking it in the air.

Some of the passengers in the centre of the rear seat, with others obscuring their view, thought the driver was receiving a reprimand. The driver, who had known May from childhood, thought so too. He lifted his hands from the wheel and raised them palms upwards and swung around to look for an explanation from Amy. But Amy had shrunk in her shame and misery between a small boy bearing signs of car sickness and a man bearing signs of a traveller in tea, for his attaché case was across his knee and he was utilizing travelling time by going through papers.

In spite of herself Amy was impressed by an illustrated spill of tea from one corner of a sheet of paper, the leaves growing fainter as they crossed the page. She wondered if she might get to know the man, perhaps he would find her a job at the place where he worked. There would be jobs for a lot of people surely, because of all the tea sold. She had a swift vision of the big brown enamel teapot in May's kitchen, nearly always full and hot, and felt her chest and throat begin to tighten. She decided to imagine a handsome tin of tea which she would send home as a gift. She saw Kathleen and Patricia bent over it, only their backs showing. Lebby was in May's arms looking down on it too, her eyelids lowered.

Amy and the man exchanged one glance. His eyes were cold and a pale grey with very pale lashes and sandy brows that grew in a little tuft near the bridge of his nose and didn't bother going further. Amy looked again to make sure she wasn't mistaken. She thought there must be hairs above his eyes, too faint to see clearly. But there were none, only skin shining and faintly blue, stretched tight on the bone without flesh to nurture growth.

Amy looked away from the glare of his unfriendly eyes. Oh my goodness, she thought, up till now I've only seen one kind of eyebrows. There must be a lot of things I haven't seen. An excitement crept in faint shivers from her thighs upwards to pump her heart harder. I'll see things, I'll do things! Keep your old job in your tea factory! The farm houses flew past, the cows leaving bails in bored little knots, the dead timbers of great trees white against the green of grass-covered hills. Goodbye to all that! Amy ran her hand down her side raising a buttock, tucking her skirt under it, no longer touching the tea man.

"Pardon *me*," she said, and the small boy in spite of advancing further into his state of squeamishness raised respectful eyes to her face.

Nearing Sydney, Amy had begun to worry, aware that she must leave the train at Central Station and find her way to Annandale. She left her case in a locker at the station (wishing she did not have to spend money this way) and took only her handbag and a bag crocheted from string, a method taught her by a hotel guest, and inside this wrapped in brown paper a nightdress, toothbrush and hand towel. Her aunt would surely allow her to stay overnight and a few subsequent nights until she found work and a room or board somewhere cheap. Sydney was cheap, she knew that, and there was proof of it visible from the tram she was riding in—a great sign on the side of a building that said three-course meals for sixpence. One of those meals a day would be all she would need, with a cup of tea and a slice of bread and butter for breakfast and a twopenny pie at midday. That would mean eating for ten shillings a week, and if she got a room for ten shillings there would be money over from her wage (she hoped for thirty shillings) to buy some clothes. She had to jerk her thoughts away from clothes, remembering a pleading promise to send things home for the little girls when May shouted to her about their thin jumpers and the absence of warm singlets for the winter.

She had asked the tram guard to tell her when Wattle Street came up. Intrigued by her big blue eyes, he hovered near her and put on an air of authority, giving tickets and change with a flourish and saying "Fares, *plis*," even when he was aware there were no new travellers on board. All of it was put on to impress Amy, a girl from the country as she had told him, who might be seen on the tram again and would be good for a squeeze of the hand when they exchanged money, nothing more, him a married man with four children and a good Catholic. He snapped his bag open and shut for nothing, then when the tram started up after a stop, he held up two fingers and she didn't know what he meant and looked frightened, which gave him cause to bend over and say he meant there were two more stops before she got out.

A nice man, Amy thought, gripping both her bags tightly in case she left them behind. People were helpful in the city, they minded their own business too, as she had been told by travellers through Moruya. Amy looked for verification around the tram but saw only solemn and frowning faces, many of them pinched looking, wedged between shabby hats and coat collars. They are hungry for their tea, Amy thought generously, wondering what hers would be. She stood now, for the guard had given her another signal. I know he's sorry to see me go, she thought, feeling loved and wanted and happy so far with Sydney.

But number seventeen did not look welcoming, not being favoured with a street light close by and looking resentful of this, crouching dimly with only a faint light showing behind the glass top of the front door like an orange in a fog.

More light came from a May bush near the front gate, scattering petals on the path as the wind rushed about it, reminding Amy of the shower of confetti two giggling young cousins threw on her and Ted when they walked out of All Souls. She shook the memory off as the May shook off the surplus blooms, finding a bell to press and hearing slippered feet growing more distinct as she waited.

"Aunty Daph!" Amy said, squashing her crochet bag in both hands.

"My goodness me!" cried the woman, who looked a lot like May. She peered around Amy, looking for children, and appeared greatly relieved there were none emerging from the gloom.

"Come in!" she said, so heartily that Amy felt she would be welcome to stay forever. At the end of the hall was a large room where food was cooked, meals were taken and the laundry done. A small space had been left for a bathroom, otherwise this room occupied the entire rear of the house. Daphne's husband Dudley and the two sons were at the dining table, and a knife and fork were crossed on a plate of curry and rice where Daphne had left her place. Now she was pushing the plate along and setting a place for Amy, who had put her bags on the sofa, a twin to the one at home in Diggers Creek (for the sisters had got one each from the parents' home after they died). Amy was sad at the superior condition of Daphne's sofa, for Kathleen and Patricia (and Lebby, Amy supposed, though she had never seen her there) rode the high rounded end of theirs for a horse and scuffed the leather where their toes kicked it.

The stove and a big pine dresser occupied the kitchen corner and next to the dresser were laundry tubs and a large enamel gas copper. Amy knew from Daphne's letters to May that hot water from the copper was carried into the bathroom, Daphne giving details of changes, particularly improvements in her domestic arrangements whenever they occurred. She had written of the convenience and ease of lighting the copper, and told of its endless supply of hot water, bringing on a bout of discontent on May's part, out of which she eased eventually, claiming Daphne needed all the warmth available to compensate for the coldness of Dudley.

The laundry tubs were disguised when not in use by a board, covered with the same brown linoleum that was on the floor, and laid across their tops. This was used as a serving bench at mealtime, and Amy saw a rice pudding there in a dish shaped like a bed, the brown wrinkled skin like a bedcover. It made her wonder where she would sleep that night.

Daphne was at the stove pushing pots together over gas rings and lighting them with a flare of blue, a hiss and a roar.

That's gas, Amy thought, I'm seeing it for the first time. But she wished that Daphne did not look so much like May, with the same round fussy bottom and twitching apron strings. She brought a plate of curry and rice for Amy and pulled up a bentwood chair by spinning it on one of its featherlight legs.

"You here for a holiday?" Dudley said, making it sound more of a statement, not strictly requiring an answer or any continuity of conversation. He looked not at Amy but at her plate and she was afraid he might have wanted another helping and she had deprived him of it.

"There's rice custard," Daphne said, part soothing, part irritated.

"Just like Mum," Amy said. "She always cooks rice for the curry and uses up the rest for pudding."

The elder of the boys, nearly seventeen, smiled at Amy as if she were kind in saying something he could understand and appreciate. He was apprenticed to a bricklayer, having been so poor a scholar that Dudley and Daphne took him from school the day he was fourteen and found him work in the building trade, deciding that since he was big and strong and without brains, the right place for him was dealing with materials of a similar kind.

Daphne was at the tubs now spooning out the pudding. John was watching her, keen for a good helping. The other boy, Peter, a schoolboy still, kept a shy face on the dessert spoon he was fiddling with.

Peter was going to be a teacher, Amy knew from Daphne's boastful letters to May. The thought made her recall May's scornful reaction (though she did not put her views on paper), spurred on by her own sons' failure to do better than become farm hands.

"Pasty faced, miserable young know-all!" May had branded the ten-year-old Peter. The only time he visited

31

the farm he stayed clear of the animals, would not look for tadpoles in the creek with his cousins, and whinged because there were so few books in the house to read.

Amy looked furtively now at Peter to see if May's description fitted him, and saw he had a gentle face with a thoughtful expression and fair eyelashes on cheeks with a light spread of freckles the same colour as his thick thatch of hair. She decided May would not be able to describe him in her old way, and then she felt a small smile start up for she knew how May would want to, more as an insult to Daphne than to Peter.

"Your uncle wants to know if you are here for a holiday," Daphne said, more curious than Dudley, and covering it with a phony concern that he should be answered.

"Oh, sorry," Amy said, and laid her knife and fork together on her plate which was lightly smeared with brown sauce from the curry along with a few grains of rice. Amy had read that it was good manners to leave a morsel of food on your plate, not eat it clean, and she used to watch guests at the hotel to see who observed this rule of etiquette. She wove little dreams around those who did, and who crumpled their serviettes beside their plates, and left her to pick up dropped cutlery. She imagined the young men pursuing her frantically with offers of marriage (she mostly forgot she was still wed to Ted).

"Actually," Amy said, making sure she met no one's eyes. "I'm here to get work."

Spoons clinked and there were swallowing sounds, John's quite loud causing Daphne to look severely at him, though Amy felt part of the look was for her.

No one spoke so Amy did. "I know it will be hard."

"The girl next door got a job in labels," Daphne said. "She was four months waitin'."

"What's labels?" Amy asked.

"Don't youse have them down there in the bush?" Daphne asked, only slightly playing down the scorn.

John with his round shiny face gone red reached out and touched the handle of a jug, fawn coloured with a deep brown glaze near the top threatening to outshine John's eyes.

"The people bring the tops of the tea packets to her and she counts them," said Peter, taking the responsibility for explanation. "She got us the jug for all Mum saved."

"She's a great counter," John said.

Peter dug him with an elbow.

"She's got a bloke."

John beamed around them all, as if this added to the thrill of conquest.

"Mum saves the labels of our tea too," Amy said. "But she has to post them away." The silence following might have said here was another reason to escape the backwardness of Diggers Greek.

I will get it over now, Amy thought. "I was wondering, Aunty Daph, if you could put me up for a few days."

"Yes, sir!" John cried raising an arm. Having failed throughout his schooldays to raise a hand to answer a question in class, he took every opportunity of doing so now to make up for the humiliation of having to remain still and silent in a sea of waving limbs and vibrant, confident voices.

Daphne reached across and slapped his ear. "How many times have you been told to stop that silly habit?" she shouted.

Dudley got up from the table.

Men always walk away, Amy thought. Ted did, Gus does and here is Dudley going. She watched his back pass through the door for he was going into one of the rooms off the hall, the one furnished as a sitting room. Amy glimpsed it on the way in, overfull of pieces, the edge of a piano nearly touching a table of photographs, window curtains not able to hang freely since they were not clear of the table and brushing an upholstered chair jutting well towards the centre of the room, and a lounge and two matching chairs fitted around the remaining walls, and a cabinet wireless as well. There might have been an illusion of space if the centre of the carpet square had been free of clutter, but there was another table there with a green fringed cloth reaching to the floor and on it a silver vase of artificial poppies, and there was a picture of the same flowers burning a square of colour into the dun coloured wall.

Dudley went there to listen to the wireless, for almost at once there was the sound of crackling and squeaking as if someone had let fireworks off in a box of mice.

Disregarding the slap and with a big smile John shook his head and looked at Amy. "He's never learned to tune it in."

Daphne gathered up the pudding plates. "Then go and tune it in for him!"

"As per usual," said Peter.

Daphne rattled the plates and Amy thought she might be pretending not to hear to avoid rebuking Peter, who was most likely his mother's favourite.

Amy helped with the washing up. There was hardly any conversation between the two women, and when Daphne had wiped down the linoleum on the tub covers, she went into a room off the hall opposite the sitting room and switched a light on there. Amy followed and when she saw the single iron bed made up with a thin quilt on top and starched pillowslips she felt a beautiful ache to her limbs, an ache to the side of her head, a creeping of the flesh of her body, loosening it against her clothes. It will be heaven lying there, she thought.

"I'll put a table for Peter to work at in here when he goes to college, and something for his clothes if I don't get any setbacks between now and then," Daphne said, turning back the quilt.

She is telling me I can't stay permanently, Amy thought, not discouraged. She removed her shoes and tucked them under the chair in the corner, one with a leg bent right under, unsafe for sitting on but handy for her clothes when she took them off. Daphne flicked the light off then on, to indicate where the switch was and the necessity to use only a minimum of electricity.

When Amy's head was on the pillow she whispered to herself. "Thank you God. Please don't punish me too much for leaving my little girls."

6

Finding work at Amy's age with no skills apart from domestic ones proved very difficult.

Daphne was up early to get John off to work and she brought the newspaper from the front veranda to Amy in bed. Amy had to scan the employment columns and note any suitable vacancies, write down the addresses and have the paper refolded to leave by Dudley's porridge plate.

"He's that fussy," Daphne said.

Dudley did not want Amy in the house, but everyone else did.

"Where is she?" John would ask when he got in, taking his old felt hat from his sweaty head.

Peter was studying for his Leaving Certificate and talked shyly to her about the poetry.

"I don't understand what it all means, but I love the sounds. Like music," Amy said.

"Me too," Peter said.

Daphne to her surprise loved having another woman in the house. As if her conscience demanded an explanation, she told it she supposed she had missed having a daughter of her own.

"I been wanting to move that couch to under the window for ages," Daphne said one day when she was mopping the kitchen floor and Amy was scrubbing down the pine dresser.

"Come on then," Amy said, and with a couple of swoops of her young body had a small cane octagonal table astride the window sill and had hold of one end of the couch.

When it was in place she took the cane table under her arm and looked about for a new place for it.

"There!" she cried, setting it down in a corner of the hall near the door into the kitchen. "As soon as you open the front door you see it, and we could put a vase of flowers there. Looks real welcoming!"

"Look at that!" Peter cried when he saw the table. "Just the place to put the books I have to take to school next day!"

"We'll leave it bare then, Aunty Daph," Amy said.

Peter flopped full length on the couch. The sun gave the brown leather the richness of blood, and the brass studs fastening the beautiful little pleats on the headrest shone bright as gold. Peter's thick fair hair shone too. The girls will like him, Amy thought.

The woman next door, the mother of the girl in labels, asked about Amy's children.

"I could never go off and leave mine, young like that." She drew down her eyebrows and the corners of her thin mouth.

Daphne tossed her head and splashed some water onto a starched pillowslip, rolling it up so tightly it looked no bigger than a handkerchief.

"It would be too cruel to take the little things from May."

Mrs Cousins's eyes swept the top of Daphne's head and rested on the top shelf of the dresser where the brown jug sat, the one exchanged for the tea labels, for which she felt part ownership. The eyes neither agreed nor disagreed with this sentiment.

"She misses them, she cries herself to sleep some nights." Daphne's eyes were steel arrows piercing those of Mrs Cousins, who began nervously to pleat her skirt across a thigh.

Daphne hoisted a basket of clothes to one end of the table to leave space for the ironing blanket. She had the pleasant prospect of Amy sharing the job. Amy liked doing Dudley's shirts and those Peter wore to school. Starched collars were a novelty to her since at home in Diggers Creek there were only rough farm clothes to iron. Dudley was a tailor who went to work dressed as an advertisement for his trade.

"I suppose no job don't help much either," Mrs Cousins said, mournful on the outside, but cheered within thinking of her Helen. Mrs Cousins had just laundered her uniforms, orange coloured with dark blue trimmings matching the tea labels. Her ironing was all done so she could sit in comfort and watch Daphne.

"There she is now," Daphne said, speeding up the iron in time with the hurry of Amy's feet coming down the hall. That speed might mean good luck at last.

But her face said otherwise. There was strain, even fright in her eyes, very large, a shine on her pale skin for the day was unusually warm for early spring. Her pert little nose shone too and perspiration had darkened her hair.

"Sit down there on the couch," Daphne said. She badly wanted to offer Amy a cup of tea but it would mean including Mrs Cousins and if her ten-year-old wandered in, as school was out, between them they were capable of emptying her biscuit tin.

"I'll get you a glass of water," Daphne said.

Mrs Cousins looked at Amy's seated body, marvelling at its youthfulness. You'd never know, she thought.

"Don't say your age," Mrs Cousins said.

"How old?" asked the man at Amy's next interview.

It was a knitwear factory in Newtown and the advertisement sought a young girl for general duties, mainly typing labels describing packaged goods for retail outlets.

The man was short with a skin that looked lightly smeared with grease. You could see hairs sprouting from little pockets of oil. There were some holes without hairs, and Amy thought of a cheese coloured a yellowish grey marked with the feet of mice.

The man's hair was lightly greased too and he had what was called a cowlick in front and yellowy green eyes, a colour Amy had not seen before. I am always finding new things on faces, Amy thought. What will I see next?

A woman about thirty came into the office and opened a steel cabinet and took some papers from it. Amusement, though very guarded, ran across the man's face. He threw a pencil about a desk pad. The redhaired woman left the room without looking at Amy. She saw me alright, Amy thought.

"I'm eighteen," she said.

She was to start work the following Monday. The pay was twenty-five shillings a week and the hours were from eight in the morning to five in the afternoon. Amy saved her tram fare by walking home after the interview. She crossed the park adjoining Sydney University, passing some students with books and dragging feet. She smiled into their faces, she couldn't help it. A job, a job, I've got a job, she wanted to cry out. Twenty-five shillings a week! Only a pound at some of the other places. She dismissed the reason, her real age, for failing to get employment earlier. She started to run down the gravel footpath as if she really had shed the extra years and was only eighteen. A child whose mother sat with outstretched legs ran in front of her to scoop up a handful of little stones.

"Keep that away from your dress!" the mother called.

Amy saw the dress was pink organdie, a bit big on the thin little girl, it was handed down from an older sister, Amy guessed, seeing it stand out stiffly, making the thin little legs look even thinner.

About Lebby's age. Amy slowed her pace and concentrated on the trams shrieking along Broadway, dismissing the look the child had given her: the watery depths of her eyes asking what right she had to run like a happy boy.

Amy walked with grown-up dignity until she turned into Wattle Street, then ran along the footpath past the houses crushed together, some semidetached, and two or three big old family homes of the past converted to flats and bed-sitting rooms. The verandas were turned into bedrooms, or sometimes a kitchenette with the main room opening into it. Canvas blinds were hung against the railings. The slightly sloping floor was usually covered with linoleum, a tattered edge often visible from the street below.

Amy looked up at these buildings with affection. She might get a little place like one of them if the rent was not too high. She knew from the newspapers that rents started at around twelve and sixpence a week. It might be possible to pay a little more for a better place and share it. She ran her mind over the faces of the girls looking her over while she waited to see Mr Yates. Perhaps one of them was looking for somewhere to live.

I will work hard, I'll be neat and particular and I won't daydream. I'll dress nicely and always clean my shoes. She looked down at them flying along the footpath and realized she was running hard now. I'll be the best worker in the place. I know I will.

7

She was as good as any. She had the small front office to herself, reached by a short flight of stairs from a door opening onto the footpath.

The job was a newly created one in the Lincoln Knitwear factory which was owned by Lance Yates and his brother Tom. They bought yarn, dyed it, and cutters and machinists turned it into clothing. The business had grown sufficiently in the past few months for Amy to be added to the staff of half a dozen clerks and typists. She would receive callers whom she would direct to a chair discarded from Lance Yates's office, while she went importantly through the main office to tell him who was there. A rack of clothing samples from the factory was against one wall and separated from this a rack of garments with small flaws sold to the public. A counter served as a desk with a heavy old typewriter at one end.

Amy had taught herself to type on a machine at the hotel. When Lance Yates got her to type a label describing the colour and size of a line of shirts, she rolled the paper into the machine, smoothed it out with a loving hand and poised her fingers over the keys with great confidence. Lance Yates admired her long supple hands, the loose joints of her fingers and deep narrow fingernails, clean and unpainted (he was dead against painted nails and would not allow them in the office). He did notice, but refrained from mentioning it, that Amy typed "grew-neck" instead of "crew-neck", and when she realized the error a few days after she started work, she and Peter flung themselves back on the couch in mirth and Daphne indulged in a little smile cutting out biscuits at the kitchen table. She is like a sister to the boys, Daphne thought, glad that Dudley was listening to his silly old cricket and not sitting there at the table with a tight mean face.

Amy helped Daphne and Peter make a vegetable garden by the back fence. Remembering Gus digging on her wedding day Amy said: "Our yard at home is no bigger than this you know." She tore at a massive growth of vines wrapped around a pile of discarded pine boxes.

"Dear me," Daphne said, both shamefaced and admiring as Amy flung the boxes aside, bruised leaves and stalks clinging to them.

Peter found a marble, a large one with colours swirled inside like the sweet known as a bull's eye.

He tossed it to Amy who wasn't ready to catch it. It hit the little bone near her throat and rolled down the front of her dress. She shrieked and dived a hand for it, bursting open two buttons. Peter's jaw dropped like the marble at the sight of a piece of breast, round and blue veined, tucked into her brassiere.

"Stop that silly nonsense!" Daphne cried and raised her hoe as if to strike him. When she lowered the hoe she trailed her eyes down Amy's front, very cold eyes, following Amy's hands fastening her buttons.

Peter went inside, returning with some books. He made a seat of an old apple tree stump.

"That's more like it!" Daphne called, hoeing hard.

"We could plant a passion vine to fill the corner," Amy said.

"We'll see," Daphne said, tearing weeds from the teeth of the rake.

Amy went past Peter's bowed head to bring the wheelbarrow. He saw her ankles above her oldest shoes, passing each other like dainty, busy birds.

He dared not look upwards to her dainty, busy bottom, feeling Daphne was watching.

That night getting the tea, Daphne managed to allow everyone a view only of her back.

She looks as if the rake is still stuck up there, Amy thought, setting the table. Aloud she said: "Perhaps I should start looking for somewhere to live."

John on the couch straightened his back, rounded his eyes and lost control of his mouth. Amy, hating herself, went to the window with a handful of forks, looking out at the debris, piled in a great heap to dry.

"That'll make some bonfire, Johnno," she said. He got up and stumped across the back veranda and down the steps. Daphne put her head out the side window.

"Tea's on the table, can't you see?" she yelled, and Dudley came in, his face asking sourly why the shouting. I have everything to put up with, grumbled Daphne to herself—the worry of the boy's big exam, Dudley never saying a civil word, the extra on the bills. Her fifteen shillings goes nowhere (though when it was first offered Daphne told Amy it was more than she expected).

"We're making a vegetable garden down the back, Uncle Dudley," Amy said cheerfully. Dudley pulled out his chair at the end of the table and sat, the noise and the movement Amy's answer if she expected one.

She went to her room as soon as the washing up was done. She knew the sight of her little cane chest of drawers would lift her spirits. It was the only piece added to the room since she had come.

Amy had been out walking one Saturday afternoon when she came upon an auction sale at a house. The furniture was piled on the small front veranda. Some spilled into the garden and a few pieces were over the front fence on the footpath. The auctioneer was standing with one foot buried in the cushion on a seagrass chair and the other caught between the veranda railings.

His assistant crouched like a monkey on the rail top. He looked a lot like a monkey too, dark and skinny, a breadboard in his little brown clawlike hands. The board against his bunched knees supported his writing pad to record the sales. The crowd expected him to lose his balance at any moment and this entertained them as much as the auction, since few of them could afford to buy anything.

He reached down and caught up the dressing-table by one of its legs. The drawers tipped open and this caused the crowd to cry "Oops!" and the young man to slap the drawers back into place. The mirror sent silvery shafts right out onto the street, and when it jerked back and forth the reflected cars danced crazily. For a second Amy saw herself streaked to a great length, quivering crazily too before the mirror was tipped to lie flat, where it blinked and flashed at the sky, attempting to outshine the sun itself.

"Here-we-have-a-lovely-piece-for-a-lady's-room!" boomed the auctioneer, his eyes on Amy. She raised a hand in acknowledgment, and the auctioneer shot a finger at her.

"Two shillings from the little lady!" he cried and everyone looked with respect and some with envy at Amy. She turned pink and ran a finger across the blue band holding back her hair, making it smooth above her forehead and bunching it up beautifully at the back. She had no more than five shillings in her purse and felt it nervously now in sudden fear that some coins might have escaped.

"Here we have sixpence over there!" The auctioneer's eyes swept beyond Amy for a moment then back to the top of her head. Amy's hand went up with the purse in it.

"Three shillings, any advance on three shillings, any advance on three shillings? Going, going, gone! This lovely little piece for a lady's bood-wor! A place for her to store her bloomers and things!"

His eyes for a moment stripped Amy to her underthings, while she blushed scarlet and looked inside her purse. The auctioneer, losing interest in Amy once the sale was made, slapped the chest, nearly upsetting both it and the skinny young man, who turned his threatened fall into a leap and handed the chest over by one leg, then took Amy's money, leaping back on the rail to be ready for the sale of a rolling pin.

Amy felt terrible making her way through the crowd. The chest was difficult for her to carry, and worst of all she could not avoid seeing her red embarrassed face in the mirror whatever way she turned it.

"Muggins!" called a fat woman without teeth who wanted the chest but had an out-of-work husband. "There was no sixpenny bid! You paid an extra bob for it!"

Amy put her face between the cane legs and ran. Oh, I do look a fool, she said to herself, avoiding the eyes of pedestrians. Oh, I shouldn't've bought it. I shouldn't've! Her purse felt terribly light, flat in her hand, reproaching her. She would have to manage until next pay day, nearly a week away, on two shillings. She would have to walk home every night. If only someone would catch up with her and say, "Let me buy that from you, here's five shillings!" She shifted the legs to straddle her hip and met eyes that asked whatever was going on. Oh, take the thing, Amy cried to herself. They will laugh at me when I get home, if ever I do!

Peter was the first to see her and ran from the veranda to open the gate.

"I saw this flashing!" he said. "It's the mirror!" He took the chest from her and bound his long thin arms around it. She ran and opened the front door for him.

"Whatever's that?" Daphne cried, coming down the hall. The little drawers answered her, running eagerly out

47

and back as Peter tipped them. He laughed and set the chest down and stood back to admire it.

"Was it alright to buy it, Aunty Daph?" Amy asked, pleased with their faces.

In her bedroom Amy set it against the wall opposite the foot of her bed. Admiring it she backed until she sat on the bed.

Daphne was in the doorway. "More for a little girl's room. But lovely."

Amy was about to tip the contents of her suitcase, in which she stored her underwear, onto her bed to transfer them to the drawers. Instead she went with bowed head and put her fingers into the open parts of the plaited cane that made a frame for the mirror. They did not easily fit but the fingers of Kathleen and Patricia would have. She turned away and smoothed the bed where she sat. Someday I'll have them with me, she thought, and it's a good idea to start getting some things together.

She looked across at Daphne, half expecting she would be reading these thoughts, but Daphne, having heard Dudley come in after watching cricket in the park, was going out pulling at the door.

"Keep this shut on it," she said.

8

It wasn't Dudley but Daphne who forced Amy to leave.

She had been several months at Lincoln Knitwear, but it seemed like years.

She always ran up the stairs to her office although she was usually early, and when she closed the flap at one end of the counter shutting her inside, she felt like a proud home owner closing her door on the outside world.

She would start rattling her old typewriter at once, for the factory began operating half an hour before the office. Waiting for her there would be a stack of paper sheets filled out by the forewoman. From these Amy typed her labels. She was often excited by something new.

"Royal blue/white polo neck", or "burnt orange contrast basque, cuffs", were enough to make her decide to fly down to the bottom floor at midday when the machines stopped and the presses ceased their great steamy sighing, and the women, still at their places, were eating sandwiches and reading from paperback novels, very tattered. They had so little time for lunch it was hardly worthwhile moving away.

Amy replenished the stock sold to the public, although she believed there could be a better turnover.

"Help me make a decent notice for Lincoln's front door," Amy said to Peter one Saturday afternoon, and checking Daphne's whereabouts (she was in the vegetable garden) he put aside his homework.

"'Seconds for Sale'," said Amy, quoting the existing notice. "You would think they were selling *time* not *clothes*!"

Together they printed in bold letters an invitation to inspect top quality goods at greatly reduced prices. *Some with Tiny Flaws*, Peter printed in the smallest letters he could make.

"That will show just how tiny they are," Amy said. She pulled her head smartly away from touching his at the sound of Daphne's feet on the back path, and he scrambled back to the table and his books.

Amy repaired some of the flaws. Lance Yates found her in her lunch hour mending a cuff where the wool was unravelled. The sight brightened his yellowish eyes, spilling a trickle of oily light over Amy's bent figure. She was intent on her stitches so did not see.

"We are not selling so much because we ask for cash," she said.

She felt sorry for the people coming in, fingering the clothes hungrily but without enough money to buy. They asked sometimes for them to be put aside on a deposit of a shilling or two. Lance Yates was adamant that there were to be cash transactions only.

"They will pay a bit off then leave it for six months and the day after we hang it up and sell it they'll be in for it.

"Besides," and tilting his head back, he quickly checked that the main office could not hear, "you have enough to do here without keeping track of other people's stuff."

His next words made Amy even happier.

He was having the switchboard moved to Amy's counter for her to operate it.

The board was proving a distraction in the main office. There was a tendency to halt pens and typewriters when other than routine calls came in. Too often June Carter, combining invoicing with operation of the switchboard, tried to handle complaints instead of passing them on immediately to Miss Sheldon. Lance was rarely in the office, but mostly supervising pressing operations, for which he had a fetish, standing over the presser and sending her into a lather of perspiration rivalling the steam flying from the machine.

Miss Jean Sheldon was twenty-nine, abandoned by a former lover, and making a determined bid for Lance's attention, though he was married with a son.

The girls in the office observed Lance's eye for Amy, and Miss Sheldon's jealous one aimed in the same direction.

Those who disliked Miss Sheldon (nearly all) were gratified (though grudgingly) by this development, and warmed to Amy when she seemed unaffected by Lance's attention.

They did not fail to observe the unnecessary trips Miss Sheldon made to the "front" as it was called, in case Amy got the idea she was not under Miss Sheldon's supervision. When Lance gave Amy an instruction Miss Sheldon often repeated it, wording it differently.

After Lance told Amy she was to operate the switchboard Miss Sheldon came to Amy with lifted chin. I always think of our old ginger cat the way that fur is coated on her face, thought Amy. Miss Sheldon ordered Amy to spend an hour a day for a week practising taking calls and putting others through to the factory.

"Yes, Miss Sheldon," Amy said. "What time tomorrow?"

"I didn't say tomorrow." Miss Sheldon had permanent creases between her reddish eyebrows. One flared up before the other, Amy always noticed.

"But Mr Yates did," Amy said.

She almost decided to take the tram home to get there quicker with her news. But she reminded herself she had no rise in salary to warrant such extravagance. Her concession to the occasion was to bound along, darting around people coming towards her. They will think me mad, she told herself, not minding at all.

Peter was often hanging over the front gate waiting for her. Sometimes John, washed and with his hair combed after his work among the bricks, sat on the step and waited too. But tonight an early gloom had settled over the house and little front garden, and their absence made it darker still. Even the light in the front glass seemed dimmer than usual.

"I'm home!" Amy called going down the hall. Daphne, setting the table, lifted her eyes then lowered them. She looks like Mum when I told her I was leaving, Amy thought, unhappy that she seemed to have brought the outside chill in with her.

Dudley did not look up from a sheet of paper he was studying, and Peter on the couch had his knees drawn up and his chin on them and was staring ahead under his floppy hair, making her feel she should wave her arms to have him notice her. John's grin was like a flag raised.

Amy slipped into her room to hang her bag on a brass hook, one of four attached to a piece of carved wood found under the house when they were looking for flat boxes to plant tomato and lettuce seeds. John had fixed it to her wall and helped her polish the hooks, and Peter had watched from the end of her bed.

Daphne had called them out sharply when Dudley asked silently, with his head cocked to one side, for an explanation of the talk and laughter.

Now Daphne was making the same gesture towards the paper Dudley held. Isn't it strange, Amy thought, that people married to each other, though so different, do the same kind of things? She wondered briefly if she had adopted any of Ted's habits. I don't think so, she assured herself.

"A nice old school report there!" Daphne cried. Peter drew his legs up even higher.

"Put your feet on the floor!" she shouted, slapping a fork down hard.

Amy knew the report to be the results of the trial examination pending the major one three or four months off.

"Only fifty-five for geography," John said.

Amy wanted to laugh.

It didn't seem such a big issue to her, not enough to paint such acute unhappiness on Peter's face. "Pooh!" she said, and his eyes met hers gratefully. "It's not the big one!"

Peter's shoulders went back as if he would be ready for the big one. Daphne slapped down another fork. "He didn't study for that exam! Is he goin' to study for the next one?" The cutlery jumped and screwed itself about and Daphne straightened it, her face dark, as if someone else was responsible.

Amy took plates from the dresser to warm them on the rack above the stove.

"I was just about to do that," Daphne said.

9

Amy was in a place of her own in Stanmore when war broke out in Europe in September 1939.

Similar to those she passed on her way to Coxes in Annandale, it was also within walking distance of Lincolns so she could save on tram fares. The closed-in balcony was her living area, but she had to go into the bedroom for water, as the only tap was over a handbasin there. Amy filled her small round tin dish and carried it to the balcony to wash her cup and plate. She used as little hot water as possible, for the gas meter had to be kept fed. Her one extravagance was to bake a mutton chop and a potato in her tiny oven.

Peter visited her one Saturday and she halved her dinner, with much laughter, serving it on her two bread and butter plates. She had an apple pie which she started to cut down the middle then decided she didn't want anything sweet and put it on a saucer at his place.

He was at Teachers' College, the one attached to Sydney University, and his scholarship gave him fifty pounds a year, much of which was given to Daphne for board.

"I nearly got a job Friday nights and Saturday mornings at Coles but there were too many after it," he said, taking very small bites so that he would not finish too far ahead of her. "But the lady said I would most likely get the next vacancy—if there is one."

That would be something I would like, Amy thought, a job in charge of people. She saw herself immaculate in a tailored suit going down the counters in Coles, looking severely on the staff whether they were serving or not, frowning more deeply if she had to straighten goods in fixtures.

No, I don't think I'd like that so much, Amy decided, thinking of her corner at Lincolns. She had a swift vision of it waiting for her. Come and be cosy here, it seemed to say. She smiled and Peter saw.

"How did you go on the switchboard?" he asked as if he had the same vision.

"Oh, I'm always wondering who will ring next!" Amy cried.

"I might ring you up," Peter said. "Would they mind?"

"You haven't got the phone on, have you?" She felt a jealous pang at missing out on such a momentous event, wondering where they would install it.

"No, from a box."

After that they talked about the possibility of war, for Peter had listened to Hitler's speech on the wireless the previous night and he thought England would come into it straight away.

"Then us." He looked at his hands, sliding the palms one against the other. She thought of them holding a gun.

"You wouldn't go though before finishing your teaching course?"

"I don't know." He got up and took his plates and looked around wondering what to do with them, since there was no sink or bench. She brought the dish, feeling sad her place was not better equipped but not sure this was the cause of her change of mood.

"Germany will round up all the young ones," he said, pleased to find where the tea-towel hung. Amy had boiled the kettle for their tea and poured the rest over their plates.

"I could walk all the way home with you," she said when they were crossing the park. But she knew by his silence he didn't want that.

He wrote to her the following week.

> I felt very mean not asking you to walk back to our place. But Mum says a lot about you deserting (that's her word) your children. Don't worry, she is guilty about asking you to leave. People are so strange. (Not you.) Classes are a bit of a bore. It's hard to settle down with so much going on. If I enlist I will tell you first.
>
> Love from Peter.

When she put the letter down on the little cane dressing-table she got a picture of his face over the tea-towel very serious, but with blood running from the forehead into the corner of his eye and down to the corner of his mouth, opened in astonishment that something was happening to him: he didn't know what.

She turned away quickly so that she wouldn't see him fall.

Peter died halfway through 1942 when Australia was at war with Japan. Daphne refused to allow him to enlist during the war in Europe.

"No son of mine is goin' to fight for that mob," she said, meaning the English.

Stinkin' Poms, she called them. She and May had lost their only brother in the Great War more than twenty years earlier.

Peter brought up the subject of enlisting on a Saturday afternoon, watching Daphne hoeing between two rows of young silver beet.

He was seated on the same apple tree stump where he had been the time he threw the marble down Amy's dress. Everything reminds me of her, he thought. Even the war. Perhaps I just want to go to war to fight for her.

He was still part mesmerized by the memory of her fishing the marble from the front of her dress. That vision gave way to another—Amy in the blouse she wore the day he went to her place and ate dinner with her.

The blouse was silky, deep blue with full sleeves, something new she'd bought. He wanted to ask her if she remembered the marble when she leaned over him with his plate, giggling at the little serve. But there she was distracting him with that column of thick cream poured into the opening for her neck. It was even lovelier than he remembered. He needed to concentrate on his chop, hoping his face did not show the heat that came there.

She was so smartly dressed in spite of being home from work, so different from the women he saw on his way up the stairs. The unfamiliar male tread brought tousled heads through doorways, old kimonos clutched to slack bosoms.

Amy had stood well back from the washing-up dish to keep her cream skirt free of splashes, and afterwards she went to the little cane dressing-table to put something from a jar on her hands and comb her hair. She is perfect, he thought. Perfect. Why is it, in a way, I wish she wasn't?

He wanted Amy there hoeing, and began to hate his mother and think how ugly she was. Ashamed, he got up and went inside and shut himself in his room. John no longer shared it; he'd moved in where Amy used to be. It looked so different now with John's old clay-covered boots lying on their sides on the floor, and the bureau he took from his old room littered on top with dogeared paperbacks and comic books. Peter hated looking in there.

He lay on the bed, averting his eyes from the table Daphne had bought him, spread with his books. He should be studying but he wanted to hold the feel of Amy's silk shoulder rubbing his as they walked through the park. He hated himself for his cowardly act in not allowing her to come right home with him. She might have been re-established as a regular visitor.

Daphne approved of Peter's enlisting when Japan came into the war even though he was through college and teaching in a school at Bondi.

He telephoned Amy to tell her he had been to Victoria Barracks that morning and signed up for military service, and he would go back to teaching a class of eight-year-olds in the afternoon. He thought (providing he passed his medical) he would start training pretty soon at a camp in Liverpool. He was told that he might not have the rank of private for too long with his higher education.

"I want to get stuck into the fighting though," he told Amy, his voice from the phone booth sounding as if he were speaking from inside an empty petrol drum. She stored this away in her mind to tell him when she saw him, hoping she could imitate the hollow ring his words had and make him laugh. She couldn't say much at the switchboard, particularly with Miss Sheldon tending to behave as if she had not yet mastered the art of operating it, and checking on her more than ever.

"Little she knows but I don't want the greasy-skinned thing within a bull's roar of me," Amy muttered to herself one day after both Lance and Miss Sheldon had

61

paid unnecessary visits. The phrase was one borrowed from May and Daphne.

Lance had removed the rack of clothes and taken down the sign from the front door. He didn't want her burdened with clothing coupons, which had been introduced with wartime rationing, and the factory was making long johns for servicemen, khaki jumpers and greatcoats, and fewer civilian things. Amy was glad. She felt guilty whenever she saw the great piles of children's clothes on the factory tables, or read details of their manufacture from invoices. She had sent home two or three parcels to May, unhappy that she was no longer familiar with the girls' measurements, imagining May's scorn if they couldn't be worn. It was more than a year now since she had sent anything.

May and Daphne exchanged more letters than May and Amy. Amy did not know what excuses Daphne used when she had moved out of the Coxes. She thought about asking Peter what Daphne said about her, or what references there were to her in May's letters, or for fresh news of the little girls, but her time with Peter was always so short it seemed a shame to spoil it with any unpleasant topic.

On his last leave from training he got away from the house in Annandale as soon as he could and took Amy to Bondi. She smiled when she heard, remembering her mind picture of Bondi Beach when she was at the hotel, thinking how much better it was seeing it with Peter. He wanted to show her the school where he taught and show her where shells had fallen, for it was only a week after the attack by Japanese submarines on Sydney Harbour, and people were taking the trams to walk about the streets in the wild wintry weather, disappointed that everything looked much the same as when they'd seen it last. A few air raid wardens in caps with badges were standing about, looking as if they would like to be questioned but daring anyone to have such gall.

Amy was proud of Peter and clung to his arm, and imagined people thinking look at that nice young soldier and his pretty girlfriend. She did not look older than him, she was sure. Her cheeks were pink with the cold and she knew the tip of her nose was pink too, but her hair did not blow about too much, since it was bound with a navy blue ribbon matching a navy jumper bought cheaply from Lincoln Knitwear because the seams did not meet properly under one arm. Sitting on her bed with her ankles crossed she had darned the hole so neatly no one could possibly detect it.

She had a deep green blazer over the jumper and a navy skirt with pleats that flew out when she turned quickly. He took her into a cafe for tea and toast. It was a long time since she had eaten properly made toast. In her room she had a wire and metal contraption comprising two sides that clapped together with the bread between them. When held over a gas flame the result was usually scorched bread not toast, and no matter how much care was taken there was always a burnt taste.

The toast the waitress served was beautifully brown, the melting butter putting a shine on the finger lengths stacked on the plate so neatly she hated disturbing it. The waitress looked with great tenderness at Peter. "Oh no," she said, shocked when he offered threepence more than the cost of the meal.

"I don't have anything much to spend my pay on," he apologized to Amy when her eyes fell on a roll of pound notes thicker than she had ever seen.

They walked about, mainly on the cliffs, watching the sea turn the brown rocks black, and hardly allowing them to get their colour back before there was another great wash sucking savagely at the crevices, and making grinding noises with the sand.

"You can't believe it," she said of the shelling, looking down on the streets with the trams like busy beetles and the dark shapes of strolling people.

She felt a great safeness because he was there. They found a little ham and beef shop open and he bought some cakes from a glass cabinet which the woman, elderly and fat, but with the same expression of devotion the girl in the cafe wore, put in a box for easy carrying.

"Let me!" Amy said, caught in the wave of reverence for him. He smiled and tucked the box under an arm. The woman, checking with dark eyes that she wasn't observed by other customers, reached under the counter and with partly hidden hands slipped a cake of soap in a white and gold wrapper into a paper bag. She closed it quickly on the smell when suspicious heads turned, and handed it to Peter. Outside he passed it to Amy.

"There's no rationing of soap in the army," he said.

"I will make it last and last," Amy said, smelling it through the bag. "And I'll put a bell on it so's I won't leave it behind in the bathroom!"

In the tram he held the box of cakes on his knee and both of them noticed a grease stain making a blot on the cardboard. He put a thumb over it and she looked out the window, and when she looked back the stain had spread further and he was trying to cover it with his spread hand. The people lined up opposite, their rows of legs making Amy think of a fence made up of odd bits of wood, fixed their eyes on the box. Amy wanted to laugh at him trying to look unconcerned as the grey turned a deeper grey. She wanted to take it from him and hold it but this would make the people stare more. In a little while there was no hope of covering the stain and a corresponding stain of deep pink spread over his face. Smiles began to trickle from eyes to mouths on the watching seat.

Amy straightened her back and cleared her throat. A-hem! it said with a deep and severe frown. Don't you dare laugh. They looked away and some kicked the wood of their seats with guilty heels. She leaned towards him and whispered. "Do you want to get out and walk the rest of the way?" No, said the shake of his head. She slipped an arm through his and a hand near his on the box.

Everyone found something else to do with their eyes.

John telephoned Amy at Lincoln Knitwear to tell her of Peter's death. It was only three months after Peter and Amy had been to Bondi and she hadn't seen him again. She received a censored letter from him, so that she was unaware he was soon to leave training camp to embark for New Guinea in a contingent of soldiers to back up forces fighting to hold Milne Bay.

The Australian victory there, the first against the Japanese for nearly a year, cheered those at home.

"Our brave, wonderful boys," said wet-eyed women, openly reading newspapers over the shoulders of others in trams.

It had caused a stir at Lincoln Knitwear when Miss Sheldon joined the Land Army. Goodness me, Amy said to herself, wondering if Miss Sheldon had any idea of what was ahead of her. How would she go behind a plough, hoeing long rows of potatoes, or feeding butting bull calves? Amy looked at her standing by Lance Yates when he made the announcement (as he did on news of the Milne Bay victory). She was in an apricot silk suit patterned with green swirls and spots and her nails were polished on her strong freckled hands. I might be surprised though, Amy thought, her eyes on the hands lightly holding silk elbows.

When everyone had gone back to their desks Lance told Amy she would be moving into the main office, and part of her new job would be to oversee the work of the other half-dozen girls.

"Oh, Mr Yates!" Amy cried out, her hands flying to her cheeks, causing Lance to frown and cock his head towards the doorway, for he wanted Jean Sheldon out of the way before this announcement was made.

His young nephew Victor, exempt from service in the armed forces because of acute bronchial trouble, was to take over from Miss Sheldon. Amy was to be next in charge, the chief invoice clerk (no more typing labels) with a desk outside Victor's office facing the others. A junior would be employed to operate the switchboard and do Amy's former duties.

"An eighteen-year-old," Lance said with a smile, "like you were when you came."

Amy blushed and began to think wildly and fearfully. Perhaps Miss Sheldon would go on the land down south where Amy came from, taking the place of boys enlisted from there, and discover Amy had been married and had three children. She would pass the word back to Lance

Yates and it would mean the end of Amy's job, and who else would give her one? She felt sure she would be dismissed without a reference for being such a cheat.

She was in such miserable contemplation of this that she almost missed hearing Lance when he said she would get a rise in pay. Oh that was wonderful! Forgetting her former fears she plunged into a dream of moving into a better place with a real kitchen, equipped with a sink and a proper stove. There was another dream she could also pursue now. She would like to rent a whole house and let a couple of the rooms. In some cases this involved an outlay of only a few shillings a week, the remainder of the rent being covered by the tenants' contributions. She realized she could not ask much, perhaps eight shillings a room, since people would have to have their own furniture. All she had for herself was the little cane chest of drawers. She thought of it sitting in an otherwise empty house and had to stop herself from smiling. But when Lance Yates had left for the back stairs which led to the factory she put her head back and laughed, then popped the little headpiece on, for the board had flashed a warning light.

Lance was not hurrying down the stairs. Listening to Amy's laugh, he felt jealous that he was not sharing it, so was close enough to hear her scream, and come running back.

The headpiece was flung down and she was standing holding her face with both hands.

"Only a cousin though," said one of the girls, pulling her mouth down at the corners and inclining her head towards Miss Sheldon as if it was she who was in need of the greater sympathy. Poor old Sheldon, thought the girl, she held the floor there for a while and then little Miss Fowler took it. The girl felt moved to bring a glass of water and place it beside Miss Sheldon's bookkeeping.

"Poor boy," said Miss Sheldon between sips. "His poor, poor parents." Miss Fowler, who had been allowed to go home, was pointedly excluded. Lance sat at the switch-board himself for the last half hour of the working day, opening his mail there. He looked down with a rare feeling of tenderness on some things Amy kept on a shelf under the counter, near the stacked unused labels—a little mirror in a pink celluloid stand and a tumbler with a comb and some hair slides. She had hemmed a piece of towelling and sewn a loop of tape to the corner to hang it from a nail. There was a piece of soap on what looked like a saucer from a child's teaset. He thought they were like a child's playthings, all of them, and Amy was like a little girl playing at being grown up. He felt cheered, a sense of familiarity deepened; the dead soldier was only a cousin, not a lover. And Miss Sheldon was leaving.

"Lincoln Knitwear!" he said brightly into the mouth-piece, his hand poised ready to flick the appropriate switch.

Amy started for home then turned and ran the opposite way to go to the Coxes. The September afternoon was dying, the grass in the park thicker now with the coming of spring, and waving about as if looking for Peter's feet, for that was where they had walked when he visited her. Daphne can't be angry with me now, she told herself hurrying, wondering why she couldn't cry. It wasn't my fault Peter went to war.

Mrs Cousins was with Daphne and Dudley, both sitting on chairs at the kitchen table, whereas John's was pushed away from it. The couch looked terribly empty, Amy thought.

"Take heart," Mrs Cousins was saying. "You lost him but he helped thousands of us to live."

She didn't think that up herself, Amy thought. She's heard it somewhere.

Dudley had an elbow on the table and his face on his hand. He changed elbows when Amy came in as if this was his way of greeting her. There had been other callers Amy could see, for there was a packet of tea on the table as well as a plate of scones, covered with a piece of mosquito netting embroidered in the corners, and some tomatoes, which made Amy think of the vegetable garden out the back, hoping for an opportunity to see it.

Daphne's tears flowed afresh at the sight of Amy. "I got no word from him," she said. Did you, asked the drowned eyes and piteous mouth. Amy shook her head. She will think me terrible for not crying, Amy thought.

She went to the bench covering the washtubs where there was a piece of steak, two onions and some carrots and the big cutting knife she remembered. She rolled up her sleeves and put a frying pan over the gas flame as in the old days when she often made the braised steak.

The doorbell rang and Daphne wept afresh. "Tell whoever it is to go away," she sobbed. John went swiftly down the hall. He is not so clumsy now, Amy noticed, hardly able to hear his tread. He came back with a small packet of tea, one quarter of a pound. He did not say who brought it, but Dudley's face asked, or rather the eyelids over his mud grey eyes, not such a different colour to the rest of his face, lifted and fell.

"Mrs Thompson," said John with reluctance and Amy thought he was quite sensitive now, a good son, and they were lucky to have him. Daphne dropped her head on her arms on the table. "Hers is safe!"

"Did the Thompson boy join up?" Amy murmured to Mrs Cousins.

"Four from this street," Mrs Cousins did not disguise the pride in her voice. Thank God I had girls, she said silently. Except for young Ernie, only eleven and unlikely to be caught up in it.

"It's a cruel and terrible time," she said, standing and touching Daphne's hair. She went out swiftly by the back door, her feet gentle on the steps, not thudding as you would expect from such a big woman.

"Come on," said Amy, bending over Daphne with her hands between her knees, as if Daphne were a child to be coaxed out of a mood.

"Where?" Daphne blew her nose. "Where can I go where he isn't?"

"Just to your room. To put on that mauve dress he liked you in."

Daphne put her hands to her throat and squeezed it.

"John will set the table and we'll have tea," Amy said.

Dudley stood and half turned to the hallway as if habit dictated he go and turn the wireless on. Daphne, likewise prompted by habit, checked the boiling potatoes and simmering braise with a glance before she allowed Amy to guide her, an arm about her waist, to her bedroom.

71

Amy brought a jug of warm water and filled the china basin on the washstand. She took a fresh towel from the bottom drawer of the wardrobe. Daphne sighed in its folds and Amy knew there was a little pleasure there. Vigorously she rubbed the parts of Daphne's hair that were damp from her wash. When she combed it Daphne closed her eyes and tears ran through her lids and over her cheeks.

"Your hair is even thicker than Mum's," Amy murmured, ashamed that she could not become infected by Daphne's tears.

Why, oh why, she asked herself, catching a glimpse of her dry, bright eyes in the mirror.

She went home after tea, walking swiftly all the way, taking her usual care as she crossed the park to avoid the shapes of men lurking under the trees away from the lights, dimmed as wartime precautions. Great shadows lay on the grass and stars were visible far up in the sky. No cloud and too cool to rain she thought, keeping from childhood the bushman's weather signs.

She passed Lincoln Knitwear, shrunken in the dark, the brass plate on the doorway sending out one small brave shaft of light. She hadn't thought about her new job there at all since she'd left for the Coxes! That surprised and pleased her. She saw it as a token of mourning to compensate for the absence of tears.

But inside her room when she turned on the light and the little chest of drawers leapt at her, she dropped on her knees before it and howled with the cane edge cutting into her face.

After that Amy went regularly to the Coxes. Dear Peter, she said to herself, quite often too, you are responsible for this. Thank you.

John was a big help when she moved into a house in the nearby suburb of Petersham. She scanned the columns of newspapers advertising houses and flats to let for weeks before the move, spending Saturdays inspecting them. This one was in Crystal Street off Parramatta Road, and she could walk from there both to Coxes and Lincoln Knitwear. It was on a narrow block with a patch of garden in front and an overgrown, neglected backyard.

I'll have you looking a lot different soon, Amy said to herself, pulling at the wild growth of convolvulus over the lavatory. A climbing rose that hadn't been pruned in years, once intended to cover a side fence, swooped the wrong way like a clown pretending to have lost his way on a stage.

Here I am making my second vegetable garden in Sydney, Amy thought one day three weeks after moving in, and looked around as if she might find a stump and Peter sitting there with his books. John was pulling grass away from the fence, showing the bottom of the palings like stained teeth.

"I'll plant wallflowers on either side of the path to the whats-is!" Amy called, pointing her fork at the lavatory. She drove the fork into the ground with great energy, anxious for a feel of the soil, thinking of a row of potatoes, remembering how Gus used to say potatoes did well in new ground.

John made a heap of the grass pulled from the fence and dumped it onto the path, and began pulling the convolvulus from the lavatory as if he was carrying out a wish of Amy's.

She was glad there were no flowers on the vine, the blue might have been the blue of Peter's eyes, pleading with her to let him live.

John had energy to spare to help Amy at weekends. His job with a building contractor for the Department of Education was lighter now with all building supplies diverted to the war effort, and no new schools going up. There was only maintenance work like repairing concrete paths and roof leaks and replacing broken windows.

John missed bricklaying. He sometimes used to draw a circle of admiring schoolchildren.

"It never comes out crooked," a boy said once, dividing his reverence between a wall and John.

John used his trowel to flick away some surplus mortar, as a chef would flick icing from his decorated cake.

A teacher standing a little way off clapped his hands to tell the boy he was out of bounds. The boy backed, still with his eyes on John's hands, following the trowel as it smoothed the filling between the bricks. John rose when he was done, putting his head to one side and not looking at the boy, though caught in the power of the boy's admiration, holding it but not acknowledging it.

The teacher called sharply, "Here, boy!" and the boy turned. This made the teacher turn away, and then the boy turned back and raised a hand to his forehead in a salute. John caught up the next brick and saluted with it.

He went with Amy to auction sales to buy a bed, a wardrobe, a kitchen table and some chairs for her house.

Reluctantly Amy closed off the main room downstairs which had a window opening onto the front garden and was obviously intended as a sitting room. Amy could not afford furniture for that. A smaller room, also on the ground floor, became her bedroom.

She let the two rooms upstairs to two maiden sisters in their sixties. The Misses Wheatley shared a bedroom and used the other as their sitting room, paying Amy fifteen shillings a week. There was a bathroom between the two rooms at the top of the stairs which was shared with Amy. Amy paid the landlord one pound seven shillings a week so she needed to find no more than at her other place, although she had to put money aside each week to meet electricity and gas accounts. The Misses Wheatley cooked their meals in Amy's kitchen and ate at a corner of her table, or carried a tray to their sitting room and sat by their window to look down towards Parramatta Road where the trams screeched along and people hurried in packs to work. They reminded Miss Heather Wheatley of sheep on their property back at Dubbo, the way they jammed together as if they needed each other's support to be carried along to whatever awaited them.

The Misses Wheatley had never worked. Before coming to Sydney they had lived on the family's wheat and sheep property. After their parents died they stayed on with their brother Henry.

Henry was forty-five when he took a wife, a woman with a small dressmaking shop in Dubbo. She was thirty-eight, widowed with two children. The Misses Wheatley handed over to the bride and groom the main bedroom which they had occupied since their parents' deaths, and went back to the one they had shared for most of their lives. The new Mrs Wheatley frowned on the arrangement whereby the children, a boy and a girl, shared Henry's old room. Henry, ever anxious to please her (and unable to see her as the domineering shrew she seemed to others) agreed that it would be a good idea for his sisters to have an independent life.

The Misses Wheatley were quite eager to go to Sydney and the ten pounds a month Henry promised to pay them seemed like a fortune. They saw themselves, after rent was paid and food was bought, giving generously to the collection at the Methodist Church on Sundays, going to the movies and on day trips to the mountains by train, going to Manly by ferry for a walk between the harbour and the sea, and having coffee and cake at a cafe. They had never had money of their own, using store accounts in Dubbo for new clothes for church and the show, never in need of evening wear for they were brought up to believe dancing was sinful.

Henry's wife sent the money at the end of each month. The Misses Wheatley had reckoned on it coming at the end of every four weeks.

Miss Grace didn't want Miss Heather to make an issue of it, and upset the source.

"We do get the money on the dot though," she pleaded.

"On the dot or not on the dot," said Miss Heather, the younger and brighter of the two, beginning to realize she was now in charge of both their lives, "there are fifty-two weeks in the year and we only get money for forty-eight."

"We can manage," said Grace, shutting out of her vision the great loaded apple tree on the farm that would keep them in puddings for weeks. They had just halved an apple bought on Parramatta Road from a dreadful little foreign man, who had tried to force them to take more, throwing his hands in the air at the ten shillings offered, slamming the till open and shut at the way they were taking all his change.

The nine shillings and eleven pence was to see the week out. Heather, eating her half of the apple carefully because of an unsteady tooth at the rear of her upper jaw, looked keenly at Grace, wondering if her pallor meant she was coming down with the bronchitis she had suffered all her life, and how she would cope with the expense of a visit to a doctor if this were necessary. Their cheque was due at the end of the week, but it could fail to arrive should an emergency like floodwaters keep Henry from getting into Dubbo to the post office. Heather automatically and foolishly looked out the window to the sky, clear and blue, and hoped for the same for Dubbo.

Henry's wife was glad to be rid of most of the old-fashioned furniture that crowded the farmhouse, and agreed to paying the cost of railing it to Petersham. Amy was nearly as excited as the Wheatley women to see it unpacked. She loved the satiny finish on the chiffonier and the slender turned-in legs of a lovers' seat, capable of supporting weighty lovers in spite of its frail appearance. Some of the little tables and cabinets Amy would have died for.

She said so to John one Saturday afternoon, while engaged in a favourite pastime, drinking tea in her kitchen.

"Perhaps they will die and give it all to you," John said, thinking of the Misses Wheatley as old enough for death to be imminent.

"Oh, I didn't mean that!" Amy cried and got to her feet and seized the tea-towel to chase him around the backyard.

He dodged behind the lavatory and she shrieked at him to take care where he trod for she had planted a passionfruit vine to cover it.

He jumped clear and flung himself on his back on the grass, his big boots at the end of his still body pointing their toes to the sky.

Amy thought of Peter, and went soberly to peg the damp tea-towel to the clothesline.

I think I'll always love him, no matter what comes, she said to herself.

What came, surprisingly, was Lance Yates.

With Amy's help he arranged a benefit night in the public hall a few doors along King Street from Lincolns. The proceeds were to be for the war effort. He hired film equipment to show scenes of fighting in the war zones and activities on the home front. Amy looked hard at the pictured Land Army girls for a glimpse of Jean Sheldon. There was none, but she saw enough to wonder how they managed to remain so well groomed, hardly a hair out of place while they tossed hay and cut cabbages.

Amy typed notes inviting all the office and factory staff, and gave them to Victor to slip into pay packets two weeks before the event. Lance had suggested a printed notice for upstairs and down, but Amy said she would like to send a personal invitation to everyone.

"I'll do them in my lunch hour," Amy said. "They'll read a notice but won't believe it means them."

All the office staff went, and several from the factory squeezed together on one of the long seats, maintaining the division between office and factory. Mr Yates, putting on his most genial manner during the interval when tea and biscuits were passed around, failed to spark them into a convivial mood. They looked much the same as they did at their machines, except that they knew where to put their eyes then. Lance made a lot of mistakes with their names and had to be put right by the forewoman.

"Well, she looks like a Phyllis and not the way I imagine an Edna would look," he said, rubbing one side of his oily face.

Edna and Phyllis looked at each other, a flash of fear and a question in each pair of leaden eyes. Were their jobs in danger, displeasing him with ill-suited names? And should they consider exchanging them? Their tea slopped about in the thick cups and biscuit crumbs were scattered on their knees. They longed to be home in their dark little slum houses, smelly with humanity and soap suds, and vibrant with the cackling sound from their gossiping mothers.

Mrs Yates came to the film evening. She was short and plump and corseted and dark, and oily skinned like Lance. Amy thought their similar skins might have attracted them to each other in the first place. She had a ripe but not healthy look and painted her face liberally. Amy was pretty sure Mrs Yates believed she was smarter looking than any of the other girls there. She had a fixed smile for everyone when the lights were on, and Amy felt that Mrs Yates felt she was impressing them with her manner, non-condescending in circumstances where she had every right to be condescending.

After the film equipment was packed in the boot of his car and Amy had washed the cups and saucers and stacked them on a shelf above the sink, Lance drove her home to Petersham.

Mrs Yates removed her smile in the car. In the back seat Amy sat with her crochet bag holding a damp tea-towel (she had remembered to take one, feeling in those times of shortages there would be none provided) and the biscuits left over from supper, which Lance insisted she have. Mrs Yates felt Lance spent too much on the film evening, war effort or not. Her uneasy feeling about Amy increased minute by minute, compelled as she was to observe her there in her pale green blouse, cream jumper and navy skirt. She knew the jumper was one from Lincolns and began to think Lance might have allowed her to take it without paying.

She flung her head halfway round, seeing Amy's straight back and her hair springing away from a green band like a portrait in a frame, for the car's rear window was directly behind her. Why couldn't she sit in the corner as others would? Mrs Yates thought, leaning towards Lance to look in the rear vision mirror and accuse Amy with a heavy frown.

"Can you see there behind you if anything's coming?" she asked Lance. He gave his attention to turning the car into Amy's street and slowed his speed approaching Amy's house. He knows where I live, Amy thought. Perhaps he's seen me in the front garden sometime on his way past.

Her face was hot and her hands gripped her crocheted bag as she got out. She knew she should ask them into the house.

"Which place is it?" Mrs Yates asked to establish that Lance did not know.

Amy pointed to the light in the upstairs window, indicating that the Misses Wheatley were not yet in bed although it must be half past ten. She hoped neither was ill, but as she looked both appeared, quite robust, to pull the blind down, one on either side. They will be pleased I got a lift home, Amy thought, already looking forward to recounting the evening's programme for them. She dismissed the show of curiosity, quick enough to see Miss Heather indicating to Miss Grace that they had looked long enough. To prove they were not of a prying nature, Miss Heather put a hand between the blind and window to lower the window another couple of inches without showing so much as an eye.

Amy went around to Lance's side. "Would you care to come in?" she said, nervous at the thought of sitting them on the two kitchen chairs and keeping from them the fact that there was no third.

"We must get home to Allan," Mrs Yates said.

Amy saw Lance's disappointed face, and shared with him a vision of his large, rather shapeless son whose one interest was assembling wireless sets and who sided with his mother in all marital arguments. Amy, along with the remaining office staff, learned this through Miss Ross who was taken into Miss Sheldon's confidence. Withholding this and other sidelights on the Yateses' domestic habits would place at risk Miss Ross's reputation as Sheldon's sole confidant. Unthinkable.

Amy was relieved for herself and sorry for Lance. He bent lower over the wheel to start the car and jerked his chin once, which she thought was the only farewell gesture he allowed himself. She went into the house unhappy, wondering that she should be, thinking she should be grateful to Mrs Yates, awful as she was, for sparing her a drive home alone with Lance. Her house seemed terribly empty too and desolate when she got inside. In her bedroom the little cane chest of drawers looked forlorn and ashamed, as if it had failed like a barren parent to produce more of its kind.

She went into the kitchen to hang up her tea-towel, hearing the ring of her high heels on the bare floors, unhappy at the sight of the closed sitting-room door. She went down the back path to the lavatory, thinking it should be inside the bathroom in the modern way, wondering where the Yateses' was.

When she was in bed she began to imagine the Yateses coming in. She closed her eyes and furnished the sitting room. She sat the two of them in large fat velvet covered chairs and switched on a lamp giving a peach-coloured glow to a little table (such as the Wheatleys had) and some magazines beside the lamp, not trash but intellectual publications like *The Bulletin*, and no romantic novels such as Mrs Yates would most likely read, but a thick book with a bookmark in it and an author's name that could not fail to impress.

She would offer food and drink from a little glass-fronted cabinet containing a bottle of sherry and fine-stemmed glasses and a barrel of wafer biscuits. She would put a match to the gas fire "to take the chill off the room", without having to consider the cost.

She raised herself to look briefly at her curtainless window before lying down for sleep.

"I'll have it all one day, I know I will," she said, and to her surprise the partly empty room did not echo the words back to her.

A year later the sitting room was furnished.

Lance paid for it.

Amy protested but he got around it. He wanted to give her a raise of one pound a week because she had become his right hand (as he termed it), but there were complications.

A raise could not be kept from Victor, who made up the wages every week. Lance, anxious to keep him in his employ because of the shortage of manpower in civilian life, had promised him the first raise. Lance knew Victor was looking out for it. He was in love with a plump little girl named Bonnie Wright, who worked in an office machinery shop farther down King Street. The girl was talking about joining the women's military forces and Victor wanted marriage before he lost her to some Army colonel (or such were his fears). Sometimes she came into Lincoln Knitwear and Victor adopted the air of a spaniel willing to be kicked, and indeed disappointed if he wasn't, while she twirled her handbag and kept her mouth stretched into a great smile. There was a cold glitter in her eyes for the audience of girls, part patronizing as well since she had snapped Victor up from under their noses, not that she was all that fussed about the victory.

"I think a lot about joining up," she said, not looking at Victor but knowing the expression he wore, the girls delighting in it too. "Do my little bit!"

"Get my little bit more like it!" cried Miss Armstrong to Miss Garter and Miss Harris in the washroom before going back to their desks, for Bonnie had come in her lunch hour from the shop. Business was slack, the owner, a Jew, waiting for the postwar boom when offices would hum with activity and he could put away forever his sign Quota Sold for Today.

Bonnie dusted the typewriters and adding machines and moved them to different angles, polished the brass doorknob and keyhole and watched the clock for the time to ask Mr Cohen what he wanted on his sandwiches for lunch. She sat at a typewriter behind a little table in one corner, for the shop had no counter.

"I'll get typists' bum without the typing," she said one day to the empty shop.

The girls at Lincoln Knitwear suspected Miss Wright was in danger of losing her job in a non-essential industry. That, in their view, was the reason for her constant threat to join the forces, a safety measure against the indignity of dismissal. She was also safeguarding herself against an early marriage to Victor.

"It'll be a little bit she'll get from Victor!" Miss Harris, combing her hair with one hand, raised the other waggling a little finger separated from the others. She watched it in the mirror pecking the air like a bird's beak.

"Ooh, you're awful, Harry!" cried Miss Armstrong, mostly called Army.

Behind Amy's back Amy was called Chook, since her name was Fowler. She smiled when she found a little note on the floor by Miss Harris's desk which read "Ask Chook for the heater".

The office was cold in winter and Amy had asked Lance for a radiator. She promised to supervise its use, only to warm the room for a couple of hours each morning, and again on very cold afternoons for the last working hours.

"Thank you! Thank you very much indeed, Miss Fowler!" cried the chorus of voices when it arrived. Amy smiled at the emphasis on her name.

They warmed one foot after another, hurrying back to their places afterwards for Amy remained at hers, her feet in beige stockings and well polished shoes crossed elegantly, not feeling the need for warmth, or stoically setting a good example by placing duty before personal comfort.

Lance suggested a heater for the fireplace in the Petersham house.

"No, no, please!" Amy cried. "I'd have to go on a waiting list to get one, and the summer would be here and I wouldn't need it. Please! The other stuff is enough."

That was a three-piece lounge suite in rose-coloured velvet splashed with brown flowers, a carpet square and a cabinet with a flap that dropped down for a writing table, with glass-fronted doors on either side. Amy looked forward to the time when she could afford some pieces of good china to put behind the glass, but did not mention this to Lance, afraid he might offer to provide them.

Amy explained the furnishings to John while he sat on the extreme edge of a chair, looking back over his shoulder at the rest of it, wanting to put it as far from him as he could. Amy, in her irritation with him, crushed herself into a corner of her chair, her bare toes tickling the velvet. I'm determined to enjoy it no matter what the silly goon thinks, Amy told herself. Sit on the blasted floor if you want to.

"Shut the door when Mum comes," was all John said.

I'll do nothing of the sort, said Amy to herself when he had gone. She went to the foot of the stairs to call the Misses Wheatley.

"Come and see my pretties!" she cried out. The Misses Wheatleys came with Grace in the lead.

"We saw it come!" she said. Heather dented her knee quite sharply under Grace's right buttock.

"We were worried it might be burglars," Heather explained.

"I'd have precious little to burgle!" Amy answered. "Except for this. What do you think?"

"It makes our stuff seem so old-fashioned!" Heather cried. She stroked a chair arm and Grace put out a foot in an old-fashioned black lace-up shoe such as nuns wear and stroked the carpet, the plainest one Amy could find, light brown in the centre with a darker brown border.

"Real carpet," Grace said.

"But I love your hooked rugs!" Amy cried. "You know I do!

"It's just a start. I'll get curtains and a little table when this is paid off!"

That wasn't totally a lie, she assured herself. She estimated six months' worth of pay rise in the furnishings. I hope it doesn't get out of hand, she worried.

She closed the door quite sharply when she went out and the Misses Wheatley, starting up the stairs, looked back surprised.

The following Saturday she opened the sitting room door ready for Daphne's visit.

I will tell her the truth, she decided, going in with a jug of wallflowers for the mantlepiece.

John came with his mother and Amy fried chops for dinner at twelve o'clock. He brought a hammer, nails and screws in the old canvas shoulder bag he carried his sandwiches in for work, to repair the casement window above the kitchen stove. Dear old boy for remembering, Amy thought, seeing it as a gesture of forgiveness for the furniture.

Daphne made it easy for her too. "John said you got some new things for the front room," Daphne said. "Don't tie yourself down with payin' a lot of stuff off, or you'll land in trouble. You might lose your job. You never know."

"Oh, it's nothing like that!" Amy cried truthfully. "I'll watch the chops and John will show you."

When they came back to the kitchen Daphne said that Amy could have the little table they had moved to the end of the hall where Peter stacked his books for school and college.

"Oh, can I?" Amy cried, in danger of injuring herself when she clapped her hands to her face still holding the cooking fork. "I've always loved that little table!"

She turned back to the stove and Daphne saw the drooped bow of her apron at her waist. She put on a carefully controlled face.

"The news from Europe is terrible. And all those taken prisoner by the Japs. Thank God he's done with sufferin'."

John on a kitchen chair cleared his throat, and stared with hunger at the window he was to mend.

"How's Uncle Dud?" Amy asked. Dudley was no friendlier towards Amy than in the old days, but she kept up a show of concern for him.

"His old cricket comes first as usual and you daren't open the paper before him!"

Amy dared not smile. But you like your mats kept straight and the blind down so as not to fade your lounge, now don't you? Amy was conscious suddenly of the way people clung to their habits to make grief more tolerable, to keep up a pretence of nothing changing, despite the intervention of death. She had not thought of Dudley as grieving for Peter. Now she saw him with his head down on his way to cricket, a miserable ache in his heart, fearful of coming upon the young men of Peter's age, gathered around the pitch. Worse still, Daphne's tight cold face said that Dudley did not miss Peter at all, never thought of him, whereas she grieved every minute of her waking life.

I am glad I am done with marriage, such as it was, thought Amy. All the misunderstandings. I would never want to be part of it again. You are lonelier married, far lonelier. I am not lonely at all. Dear little table! She transferred it from the Coxes' house to her sitting room, placing it at the end of her lounge, and pictured herself curled up drinking a cup of tea there and working with her little account book. She kept strict control of her income, buying only the plainest food, budgeting so that the rent and gas and light bills never fell in arrears. I would rather have a little table than a man, she told herself, bustling about the kitchen, cleaning up after the meal, trying to keep a smile from her face lest Daphne think her strange.

"Now let's sit down on the new chairs, while John does the window!" Amy said, leading Daphne towards the sitting room. She was crossing the hall when the doorbell rang.

Opening it she found Lance Yates there.

"Why, Mr Yates!" cried Amy. "Aunty Daph, this is Mr Yates. I wasn't expecting to see you! But come in, do come in, Mr Yates!"

Oh what a fool I sound, Amy said to herself, pretty sure her face was red. I've said his name too many times. Aunty Daphne will think something is going on. Nothing is going on!

She was relieved to have her back to them both and wished for something to do, cushions to plump up, instead of standing, feeling such a gawk.

"I've been to the factory," Lance said, sitting on a chair, showing no familiarity with it. "And I dropped in to tell you what we are planning." He gave Daphne a smile as if she would appreciate the wisdom of this course of action.

"It's quite a madhouse at Lincolns as Miss Fowler will tell you. Once work starts you don't get a chance for a private conversation all day."

"I know that well," Daphne said. "I was a machinist. That's where I met my husband. He's a tailor."

A little trickle of amusement ran into Amy's brain. Here was Daphne using Dudley's trade, allied to Lance's, to establish a bond between herself and Lance. But for no reason that she could name, she was pleased Daphne appeared to like Lance.

But what was Lance here for? To tell her of major changes at Lincolns? Selling out, closing down, her job gone? A fire burning it to the ground? Now Lance slid his eyes away from Daphne to her and she saw, as she often had before, they appeared like his skin to have a light application of oil.

"We're taking over the place next door," Lance said.

Amy knew the place. A dark little boot repair shop with a back door opening into a hall where the bootmaker lived in the two rooms opening off it. He had a small child and a wife heavily pregnant with another. They were going to the country town of Guyra in the west of the state to live with the wife's family and await an opportunity to open a bootmaker's business there. The fresh air would be good for the children after Newtown, the pale thin young man (who appeared to need the fresh air most) told Lance. The man coughed a lot, fascinating the tough slum children with the way his cavernous chest leapt and quivered under his liberally darned grey jumper, as if someone had dropped a handful of grasshoppers in there. They would prolong their visits to the shop, hoping he would have a coughing turn to enliven the errand.

But what did the Yates brothers want the shop for? A dry cleaning shop, Lance told Amy. There were no others in Newtown, and when the war was over and the men out of uniform and in suits again there would be plenty of business.

"Women will want to get away from the washtubs and get their silk dresses cleaned for them when it's safe to go out after the blackouts."

Lance made it sound a wonderful glamorous time and his oily eyes told Daphne it was the kind of life she was suited to. Daphne stroked a mauve silk thigh, glad she had chosen that dress to wear.

Amy closed the door on John's hammering. In a little while Lance stood up to go. "That's it then," he said, the businessman with no thought of prolonging the visit. Amy timidly offered tea. I've never given him a cup of tea, she thought. Perhaps I won't get it right! He refused with a smile that drew Amy and Daphne together on the lounge, cementing their relationship with a tender blessing from his eyes. They did not move, yet he seemed to have drawn them physically closer together.

Amy let him out the front door and when she closed it John made a large single bang with his hammer.

Daphne rushed to the kitchen. "So rude to bang away there and not come in and say hello to that nice man! Where are the manners I taught you?"

John put the hammer in his bag and looked for splinters of wood among the gas jets of the stove, brushing at it with his big hands.

"Oh, leave him alone!" Amy said. "Look at the marvellous job he's done on the window!"

"Just for that you can walk back with Amy's table!"

"Oh, that's too much to expect!" Amy cried, though she could hardly wait to get the table in her sitting room.

She stole a glance at John's face. "But if he does he can stay and have tea with me. We'll have a can of tomato soup between us and toast the rest of the bun loaf." Amy had bought a loaf of sweet currant bread to follow their chops.

John carried the little table across his shoulder on their walk back from Annandale.

"Oh, what an eventful day it's been!" Amy said as they turned into Crystal Street.

It was not to end there. Sitting on the steps in front of her locked door was a young man in soldier's uniform and a girl in a too short winter coat over a pale green cotton dress sprigged with violets.

It was Amy's brother Fred and Amy's daughter, Kathleen.

Amy would have found it hard to believe Kathleen was there, except that she slept beside her that night in the three-quarter bed Amy was now glad she'd bought, although a single one would have cost less.

Fred had been home on his first leave after joining the Army and had brought Kathleen up to Sydney with him.

"You came to Sydney before to join up and didn't come and see me or Aunty Daph!" The rebuke was for May, rather than Fred. Amy sensed swiftly and accurately that May's lapse in letter writing over the period was due to the scheme kept from Sydney, since given time Amy might have raised objections.

Amy looked at Fred's face for the man who must be there to replace the boy whose face hungered for change when he handed up her case to the mail car those years ago.

Fred's top teeth protruded slightly in his round face. He had a habit of running his tongue over them before he spoke, needing to bring his chin forward with the effort entailed. Amy wondered if he thought this helped in bringing the jutting teeth into a straight line.

Fred explained that he was not sure of the way to Annandale and went almost directly to camp after his medical. Then he was given leave to go home to Diggers Creek before he got a posting.

"Where to?" Amy cried, thinking of Peter who died in New Guinea without any of them being aware he was there.

"I don't know at all," Fred said, forgetting to wash his tongue over his teeth and letting his eyes rest on his big boots on Amy's carpet.

Kathleen had wriggled herself into a corner of the lounge and was stroking the velvet near her, discovering the raised edges of the rose, then raising her face to show her pleasure and compliment Amy.

Amy wondered if she was missing the old leather couch with the raised end on which the children rode. Then with a hot face she looked away from Kathleen, aware that she would have outgrown that childish game. She'll be a woman in a few years, Amy thought, seeing the sprawl of her long legs in their white socks and black shoes fastened with a strap across the instep. Will I have to buy new shoes when they wear out, Amy worried, taking her eyes away, unable to bear to look too long in case there were already signs of wear.

Fred, rolling a cigarette, hoping Amy would take note of this elevation to manhood, looked across to explain about Kathleen.

"She has to go to a better school, according to Ma."

Kathleen's young fingers dug around a rose. Only a sweep of brown eyelashes quivered agreement.

"Tell Amy," Fred said, realizing too late he should have put the word mother in somewhere. But Amy did not look to him at all like a mother.

Kathleen pulled up a sock, already stretched from its most recent pull. "I was doing the very same work as last year."

"Old Cec can't teach past sixth class," Fred said. Cecil Shaw had taught the three Scriveners who started school at seven and left at fourteen. May had sent Amy's children when they turned five. The little Diggers Creek school was a mile and a half down the road from the farm. Amy remembered the wet grass bowed across the track soaking her shoes and socks on a winter's morning as she picked her way to the school steps. The same would have happened to her daughters, to those very shoes Kathleen was wearing.

She stood up quite abruptly. "It must be time she was in bed," she said, conscious suddenly of something else to face. She had not shared a bed with anyone in a long time. Already she felt a creeping of her skin, a rejection of a body in contact with hers.

Fred went with John to stay the night at Annandale, as he had to return to camp next day. In the bedroom Amy saw that Kathleen was eager to get her case open and take out a new nightgown. The smell of flannelette rushed up Amy's nostrils, making her think of the new little gowns May had made for Kathleen, Patricia and the baby. She jerked the blind at the window up, then down, and went to the little cane dressing-table to pull the band from her hair. Kathleen saw her different in the mirror, older, her eyes larger, her face smaller. She made her case tidy before closing it and standing it against the wall.

Amy thought of suggesting that Kathleen hang what dresses were in there in the wardrobe, and take one of the little cane drawers for her pants and socks, but suddenly felt too tired to bother. She had to fight a rising anger against May, Fred, and even Kathleen, who she suddenly decided might not have been caught up in an adult's scheme, and was very likely not an innocent victim of a plan to transfer responsibility to Amy. Amy began to fuel her anger with the idea that Kathleen wanted to come to Sydney, had begged May to allow her to, that she wanted to go to high school to become a teacher, a nurse, perhaps a doctor with Amy having to devote the next few years of her life to educating and caring for her.

She moved angrily under the blankets and Kathleen shifted her body timidly to the edge of the bed, thinking Amy wanted more room, guilty that she was the cause of her discomfort.

Kathleen started at the sound of movement above the ceiling.

"By the way, there are two old women up there," Amy said. "They use the kitchen, so you will see them." She raised herself and punched her pillow and turned it over. Kathleen had a pillowslip stuffed with a sheet since Amy had no second pillow.

She settled herself for sleep before she said more. "They are very inquisitive, so don't tell them your business."

There was another long silence before Kathleen spoke. "I'll call you Amy when they are around."

"That's a good idea," Amy said. "Goodnight."

The following afternoon (it being Sunday) Amy took Kathleen to show her Lincoln Knitwear.

She walked her briskly, Kathleen's unbuttoned coat flapping about her thin dress, the one printed with violets, obviously her best. Amy thought of the clothes Kathleen would need for school, and first of all of the school she would go to. She passed one on her way to Petersham Station on the few occasions when she travelled by rail to work, once when her heels were blistered with new shoes and another time when Lance, with an air of great conspiracy, allowed her to have an extra hour at home the morning the shop delivered the sitting room furniture. She heard the shouting behind the high brick walls and hurried from it, reminded painfully of Peter.

Perhaps I'm being punished for something, she told herself, hurrying now, Kathleen plunging out to keep up.

I know what it is I'm punished for but I wish the punishment could have held off until I got my house fixed up more. I might have to get another job, one paying more. No, I can't do that because of the furniture. Amy felt a choking in her throat, a feeling of suffocation, of being stifled. She slowed her pace, swallowing and putting a hand up to grip her neck. Kathleen looked up at her, with eyes a darker blue than Amy's. She had Irish colouring like her father's and his dark, rich, curly hair.

"I could stay with Aunty Daphne, could I?" suggested Kathleen. Amy felt a sense of shock. She was reverting constantly to an image of Kathleen as the little girl she had left at Diggers Creek. This leggy clear-eyed girl tuned into Amy's brain as if her own was wired to it.

"No, you can't!" Amy cried, not wanting to be brusque, but putting it down to all her worries.

"It was awful for me when I was there with Uncle Dudley!"

"Granma said about him," Kathleen said.

"What did she say about him?" I don't really want to know, said Amy to herself, but it's hard to find things to say.

"He's grumpy most of the time," Kathleen said. After a while, flinging her chin up towards Amy she said: "Does it matter?"

Amy gave the first warm laugh since Kathleen had come and Kathleen, pleased, leaned close to her as Amy walked now in more relaxed fashion for they were nearing Lincolns.

My goodness yes, Amy thought, I will have to start sorting out what matters and what doesn't.

"There it is," she said when Lincolns came up.

It was not much to see, and Amy with the swift thought that Kathleen might not be impressed, felt afraid to check her face, in case her expression said so.

The brass plate on the front door was not as bright as when Amy used to polish it. The bay window (for the buildng was once a private home) was frosted over to keep the sight of women at work from passers by, but more importantly, in the view of the Yates brothers, to keep the women's eyes on their machines instead of straying streetwards.

Amy felt cheered at the sight of the bootmaker's. It seemed to look different already and to have edged closer to the factory.

"We're taking that shop over," Amy said. When Kathleen was silent Amy explained that there would be machines in the back rooms for cleaning and pressing people's clothes that couldn't be washed.

"It will be so good when the war is over," Amy said.

"It will be terrible if Fred gets killed," Kathleen murmured. She moved closer to Amy, the sleeve of her coat clinging to Amy's sleeve as if she were clinging to Fred as long as she could.

"He won't be," Amy said, ashamed that she would miss him hardly at all, whereas Kathleen would suffer, perhaps as she herself had done when Peter was lost.

They stopped in front of the bootmaker's window, seeing shoes turned on their sides, heels and half soles in rough little heaps, a great deal of dust, a heavily rusted shoe last, some tins of polish bowled about and coming to rest in any old place, a shoe brush with the bristles worn to the wood in one corner and an old rag doll streaked on its grubby body with tan boot polish. The doll belonged to the bootmaker's two-year-old child, who sometimes sat in the window when the mother went shopping farther down King Street where the butcher's, grocer's and fruit shops were. To ease the pain of separation the child was allowed to play in the window and watch for her return.

Amy turned away at last to look at the space where Lance left his car and realized she had brought Kathleen not so much to see Lincolns, as in the hope that Lance might have returned on the Sunday afternoon to have a look again at the bootmaker's shop. She might then have taken the opportunity of introducing Kathleen as a younger sister.

He might call at Petersham again and John and Aunty Daphne might happen to be there too, Amy worried.

On their way home Amy took Kathleen's arm, lightly so as not to make it too obvious she was courting support.

"I would never have got my job there if they knew I had children," Amy said.

She felt Kathleen's arm stiffen slightly and tightened her hold.

"Granma said that might be so," Kathleen answered.

Well, did she, Amy thought. Much she knows about it! She put aside May's care of her children, years of it now, and felt only anger that her life was upset just when she was starting to enjoy it.

They were making their way to the railway station for Amy had decided on taking the train. It would be Kathleen's first ride on an electric train. When they alighted at Petersham on their way home they would pass the school and see what kind it was from the wording on the brick wall. Amy did not know if it was for young children or a high school.

"It's for kids up to sixth class," Kathleen said reading the sign. She did not totally conceal the scorn in her voice.

In a little while the scorn drained away, her face shrinking with the anxiety taking over.

"Perhaps I could go there tomorrow, and ask about the high school," Kathleen said.

"Could you find your way?" Amy asked, relieved at the possibility of her day at Lincolns following a normal pattern. She had the odd and foolish notion that once she was at her desk there would be nothing other than her work to contend with, no problems apart from that.

"Of course," Kathleen said, looking back swiftly at the school.

To her surprise Amy thought about Kathleen all the next day. Kathleen sat there at the edge of Amy's brain while she worked with her invoices and accounts, seeing a new girl who was to start as a presser, working out the difference between her age and Kathleen's, while taking her down to meet the forewoman. Lance was at the far end of the factory with Tom, examining a freshly dyed fabric by holding it up to the light. Amy wanted him to see her, yet was afraid he might. She hurried back to her desk, finding it a little less the cosy refuge it had always seemed.

She listened for the end of the day. Tom switched the machines off, their whine dying away, replaced by the run of feet up the back stairs, past the office, tumbling down the flight to the door. A young woman named Dorothy, lame in the left leg, was last.

Her feet were like a clock ticking out the last minute of the working day. Sometimes the foot of the afflicted leg scraped the stair. Amy winced with the scrape, imagining pain.

She had thought in bed the previous night she would hate the end of work on Monday, having to face going home, wondering about Kathleen, angry at the changes. She had always loved putting her key in the front door and having the hall rush at her and seeing the sitting room door, left open since she got the furniture, looking as if it had waited all day for her return. She would dash in just to pat a chair back, then tumble her things on the kitchen table for her solitary meal, sometimes a slice of ham carried home folded inside greaseproof paper, a gherkin and beetroot from a glass jar on the counter of the ham and beef shop. She would boil a potato while she took off her good clothes, then set the table with a check tablecloth made from a remnant of material bought from Anthony Horderns shopping one Friday night with Daphne. She had the kitchen to herself which she liked; the Misses Wheatley were usually out of it by the time she got home. Normally they only boiled a kettle of water there, carrying their teapot upstairs where one of them had set out some paste sandwiches and two bananas on a heavy silver tray their sister-in-law had despised.

Amy made her own meal as attractive as possible, whipping her potato as smoothly as May and Daphne did. She had planned to buy a table runner to embroider during her lunch hour, for the table Daphne gave her. She had a chocolate box of stranded cottons carefully bound on cardboard on her wardrobe shelf to work the design.

Well, nothing like that is happening tonight, she told herself, hurrying up Crystal Street. Then she began to think of Kathleen with a rising excitement. Which of her meagre supply of dresses had she put on? What had happened at the school, what was happening tomorrow? In her excitement, she squeezed the little parcel of four sausages she'd bought for their tea.

Perhaps I have missed having company without realizing it, she thought, pushing open the gate.

Kathleen was nowhere to be seen. Amy looked around the backyard and into the downstairs rooms. Jabbing her green jacket on a coat-hanger to put in the wardrobe she heard noises above the ceiling.

She's up there I reckon, Amy thought, already frightened, hurrying up the stairs.

Kathleen was in the Misses Wheatleys' sitting room on one of the hooked rugs, legs bent inwards from the knees, playing with a set of chipped marbles in the space. She had a little cotton bag, made on May's machine, into which she tipped the marbles and tightened the top.

She looked up at Amy, her mouth part open. "It slipped out," she said.

Amy knew at once. The Misses Wheatley had been told that Kathleen was Amy's daughter. The stiff maiden lady faces had so far received the news, it was settled there, spread across their skins, milky with a blue tinge smeared with pink running from the edges of the eyes upwards across the forehead. It was making its way to the Misses Wheatleys' brains.

"I don't want you bothering the Misses Wheatley," Amy said. She stretched out a hand indicating Kathleen should get up and come downstairs.

"She's no bother," said Heather, a brief blinking of her eyes saying it was Amy who did the bothering. Some late afternoon light came through the window, darting at the edges of her gold-rimmed glasses. Amy turned from the sharp little needles and Kathleen followed her downstairs.

"You can set the table," Amy said, deciding to stay calm and think what to do next while she cooked the sausages.

"Sausages!" Kathleen cried, seeing them. "Wait till I tell Granma!" She saw hope run across Amy's face. "In a letter I'll write."

She swung her marbles in their little bag like a hoopla she was about to toss at a target. "I'll put my jacks away first!" Her running feet were like little hammers hitting Amy's brain.

Over tea Amy said: "You haven't met Aunty Daph, yet. We might go there after we wash up." The sausages had cheered her, and Kathleen too ate hers with relish, carefully taking a small portion at a time with each forkful of potatoes so that the potato wouldn't outlast the sausage.

"School tomorrow, don't forget," Kathleen said.

Amy waited.

"I went to that school we passed." Kathleen dipped her head with the effort of clearing her mouth of her chewed food. Her cheeks were pink and her lashes were down. Amy saw she was pretty. She's clever and she's pretty, Amy thought, frightened, fingering her hair, thinking of her looks, looking about for a reflection of them, partly glad there was nothing to provide one.

"I saw a teacher there and he told me where the high school was and I went there and looked at it.

"It sounded like millions of kids there," Kathleen said.

She was now at the end of her plate of food. Amy worried that she might still be hungry. There was some jam in the cupboard, some bread too, but it was needed for breakfast. If Kathleen went to school Amy would have to pack her lunch. She had saved some money from her wages, looking to the time when she and Daphne might shop together for some curtains for her sitting room. In spite of her low wage and frugal life style, Amy always had a few pounds in a compartment of her handbag, in case she should fall ill and be unable to work for a week or maybe longer. She could see the money going now on extra food and perhaps clothes and books for school. She felt defeated, cheated. She wanted her old life back. Kathleen stood and lifting her skirt drew a little roll of pound notes from under the elastic of her bloomer leg.

"Fred gave it to me. For school, he said."

She sat again on her chair swinging a leg, lightly dragging the toe of her shoe across the floor. Amy was able to control her irritation because of the money.

"You have to go with me, the teacher said." Kathleen pulled her sock up tight. It seemed a habit for moments of tension.

That would result in Amy being an hour or more late for work, the office girls speculating on why, their work suffering, Victor's long face poked out his office door staring from time to time at her desk, expecting it to give out some explanation. She could telephone first from a box she supposed, but she would be better employed getting the business of enrolling Kathleen in high school over as quickly as possible, then taking the first available train to Newtown. She would make an excuse for being late, say she had to go to a dentist to have a tooth stopped, or make a long-distance telephone call to relatives because of family illness.

Amy had made only one such a call in her life. She had gone with the Misses Wheatley to the post office one Saturday morning after they had received a letter about their brother Henry in hospital with a badly cut leg, a mattock having taken a bite at it while Henry was fencing. The Misses Wheatley, greatly agitated since they were brought up to place their brother's health and welfare above their own, almost tumbled down the stairs in their haste to seek Amy's help.

She whipped off her headscarf and apron while she suggested they telephone the farm and speak to Henry's wife. Amy said she would book the call for them.

"Then all you have to do is to ask how he is," Amy said soothingly.

The Misses Wheatley, looking doubtful of their ability to do this, trotted one on either side of Amy to Petersham Post Office. Heather was able to interpret through a conversation with Henry's stepdaughter that Henry was coming home from hospital that morning, and in fact her mother had taken the farm truck to collect him.

The spirits and appetites of the Misses Wheatley returned with their enormous relief, and when Grace turned pale and moist of skin on passing a baker's shop, Amy, feeling young and strong and capable, and grateful for these qualities, bought half a dozen little jam tarts.

She sat the Misses Wheatley in her sitting room and made tea for them all. The eyes of the Misses Wheatley shone behind their glasses, particularly those of Miss Heather. She had spoken on the telephone over all those hundreds of miles for the first time in her life, and if she had to do it again, she would know how. And the tea and tarts would do them until their five o'clock tea, if they took a few good drinks of water between now and then. That would help make up for the cost of the telephone call.

"Anything we can do for Miss Fowler in return we will be only too glad to, won't we Grace?" Miss Heather said around the pastry crumbs.

Amy stood suddenly and swept her plate and knife and fork to the bench where she washed up. She would ask the Misses Wheatley to go with Kathleen to the school. She would write a note for Kathleen to give to the headmaster and tell her to introduce the Misses Wheatley, saying they lived with her mother who was unable to bring her to school. The Misses Wheatley would act as temporary guardians of Kathleen. There would be plenty of schoolchildren placed in similar circumstances, Amy decided. Soldier fathers away fighting, mothers having babies, unable to accompany children to start new schools. There was nothing at all unusual about the idea.

Kathleen dreamily scraped a foot on the floor and kept her eyes on the open kitchen door and the high fence against the back path, the division with the neighbouring house.

Bring your plate here to be washed, said the jerk of Amy's chin over her shoulder. Kathleen took it up and laid it with great gentleness by the dish and tray.

There is something quiet about her, Amy thought. She doesn't bang and clatter like May and Daphne. And Amy steadied the energy with which she worked.

Kathleen took a tea-towel and wiped up, her face tipped to one side and her eyes down.

The Misses Wheatley, on their chairs by the window, were in mourning, following the revelation of Kathleen's background.

"Oh, my goodness me!" Miss Grace said a dozen times.

"I still can't believe it!" Miss Heather said. Mostly they played a few hands of euchre after their tea, but tonight the cards were still in the little box their grandfather made from the first tree felled on their farm, which their sister-in-law had been glad to get out of the house. The box sat on one of the little tables, looking as if it would remain there unopened throughout the evening, indeed throughout the rest of the Misses Wheatleys' lives. It might have been part of a sinful past.

"Misses Wheatley," said Amy, sitting down on one of the little chairs she had always admired. "I want to ask a favour of you."

113

Both women stared at Amy's hips as if she had revealed them for the first time. Their expression said the hips had cheated, deceived them.

"I was wondering if you would walk with Kathleen to her new school tomorrow?"

Miss Heather came forward on her chair and Miss Grace moved back, Heather with a sliding movement, Grace with a jerk.

"I'm sure I don't know how we could," murmured Miss Heather.

"You know how you pass the big school on your way to the station?" Amy said. A shaft of light from Miss Heather's glasses darted to Miss Grace's and back again.

"Well," Amy went on, "you turn the first corner and the high school is right there. The back of it joins the other school."

"There was no high school for us at Dubbo," said Miss Grace Wheatley.

"Neither was there one for me at Diggers Creek," Amy said. "But there is one for Kathleen."

"Poor little thing," said Miss Heather, looking at the hooked rug where Kathleen had sat.

Amy stood and the Misses Wheatley focused their attention again on Amy's hips. She smoothed them and they took their eyes away as if she had suddenly undressed.

"Well?" Amy put her head to one side, watching the flutter of the Misses Wheatley, like hens disturbed as they were settling on their roost. "If you will, Kathleen will be ready at a quarter to nine." Amy heard her own steps brisk on the stairs, and as always thought of the carpet she would like there, but now would probably never have.

"If they don't go with you," Amy said to Kathleen when they were in bed, "can you go by yourself—with a note?"

"We were going to Aunty Daphne's tonight, I thought you said."

"Aunty Daphne can't take you to school at that hour!" The dark made Amy's voice sharper than she intended.

"Will I have to pretend the Wheatleys are my grand-mother—one of them?"

"You don't have to pretend anything!"

"Goodnight Amy," Kathleen said.

19

The Misses Wheatley did not take Kathleen to school.

Miss Heather came to the kitchen door while Amy and Kathleen were eating breakfast, and Amy knew at once there was a big change in their attitude.

Although the sisters had free access to Amy's kitchen, and they had never hesitated to enter before, Heather rapped lightly but firmly on the partly open door.

Amy did not smile at her.

"Grace is not well this morning," Miss Heather said, avoiding the blue shaft from Kathleen's eyes. "I'm sorry we can't go to the school." She fixed her gaze on Amy's saucepan on the stove, used for warming milk for Kathleen's cereal, a wheat-based biscuit from a packet, more enticing than May's porridge. Kathleen would have relished it more but for the anticipated trauma of starting a new school.

"Miss Wheatley would be alright by herself, I should think, for the short time you would be walking to Station Street," Amy said, her cold eyes on Miss Heather as if she were the junior at Lincolns, asking to leave work ten minutes early to meet some cousins for a movie matinee, because one of them was a sailor with shore leave.

Miss Heather shook her grey head, and Amy got up suddenly and moved her chair with an angry scrape of the legs on the floor.

"If you would like to move out of here Miss Wheatley you are free to do so," Amy said.

"I didn't say anything about moving, Miss Fowler."

"You can say Mrs Fowler if it makes you more comfortable," Amy said.

"Oh dear me, I don't know what to think," murmured Miss Heather, clinging to the doorknob and looking back into the hall as if for reassurance that it had not vanished. Amy was at the bench now, energetically stacking her cup and saucer and plate in the washing-up dish, and Kathleen was scraping her plate free of milk-soaked crumbs hoping the noise was not too loud. She took it to the dish and allowed her body to gently touch Amy's.

"I can go by myself," Kathleen said, "if you write a note." Amy swept the cloth from the table and flapped it not quite towards Miss Heather Wheatley but near enough to send her trotting towards the stairs.

At midday Amy decided she would not spend time eating but would take a train to Petersham, walk to the school and with luck be back by the time her lunch hour was up.

She walked very fast, pulling her green jacket on as she went, slapping her navy blue handbag, making sure her money was inside. I am spending more than I should, Amy thought. All these fares. But it can't be helped. All the morning she had carried in her mind a picture of Kathleen's small anxious face, quite pale, desperate for acceptance.

I just want to make sure she is alright, Amy said to herself, running down the steps at Petersham Station, grateful to see by the clock a good half hour to fit her errand in.

The school was out for midday too. There were children everywhere, all girls. They looked alike, all in navy blue box pleated tunics, blazers and black shoes. Amy felt a sense of panic that she would not be able to pick Kathleen out, then remembered she was wearing her violet printed dress and overcoat.

After a while she saw her on a stone step alone eating a sandwich, one that Amy had made that morning, fitting it into her coat pocket.

Amy saw the other girls' school cases sitting about the playground like brown birds resting in groups, some with a proprietary foot resting on them. Amy felt a pang for the isolation of Kathleen without school case or friend, and rushed towards her. The chatter trailed off as she passed the clumps of girls, their eyes linked her with Kathleen and a teacher dressed in a mannish suit and high-necked blouse grew more mannish, staring hard at Amy. It was plain now that she shouldn't have come, and she sank down on the step beside Kathleen feeling she might be less of an embarrassment there.

"You said Dear Headmaster on the note," said Kathleen, accusing and mournful. "It's a girls' school and it's a headmistress."

"You should have told me!" Amy cried.

"The man at the other school didn't say it was a woman!" Kathleen looked at her sandwich as if the last thing in the world she wanted to do was to finish it. "I wish I'd never come!"

Amy felt a jolt inside her. A swift vision of Kathleen with her suitcase at Central Station was sliced sharply away.

"It's just the first day," Amy said. "I've thought of something. Tonight we'll go to Aunty Daphne's and ask if she will give you Peter's school case. I think she will."

Kathleen was reminded of the money from Fred and took it from her coat pocket tied in a handkerchief, which she unknotted and counted the pound notes.

"They pinch things here," she said retying the knot much tighter and looking up under her hair to see if anyone was watching.

"Then let me look after it!" Amy said.

Kathleen shook her head and crushed the last of her sandwich into her mouth. Amy too felt the money should stay with Kathleen, binding her to the course ahead. To pass it over, even temporarily, would be a pointer to defeat.

"I can't stay too long," Amy said, standing and looking past the clusters of girls to the gate.

"You mightn't be supposed to come," Kathleen said. She made the paper bag that had held her sandwich into a tight little ball and Amy put a hand out for it.

"I had to do this real hard work by myself at the end of a desk of awful kids," Kathleen said. "They'll tell me this afternoon which class I go into.

"Probably with the duds."

"Oh, nonsense!" said Amy briskly, as if she were talking to a new girl at Lincolns who claimed she couldn't answer a telephone.

"You don't know anything about me," Kathleen said and dropped her head close to her knees.

"I have to go," Amy said abruptly, and only partly conscious of the glowering expression on the teacher's face, made swiftly for the school gate.

She trembled through the afternoon's work, not even grateful that an obliging railway timetable had got her to Newtown with several minutes to spare.

She drank a glass of water for her lunch.

A drink of water, Amy thought, putting the glass with her other things that used to be under the counter in the outer office, but now occupied a paper lined drawer with the addition of a tiny bottle of Evening in Paris perfume John gave her for her birthday.

I won't let her see that perfume, she will want it. And Amy slammed the drawer shut and shut out the angry picture of Kathleen eating a sandwich she didn't want, while Amy's throat craved for one. She saw herself drinking water for the rest of her life while Kathleen ate.

Lance came into the office in mid-afternoon with details of a big order for Air Force overalls worn by mechanics doing maintenance work on aeroplanes. His eyes shone.

"The next thing will be the uniforms, the real thing!" he said. Amy in her troubled mood had the impression that Lance wanted the war extended in the interests of business. She lifted her eyes from the typewriter just enough to see his yellowish fingers curled around the invoice, clinging to the triumph.

Oh, I feel so terrible about that furniture, Amy thought. Every time I see him I feel I should say something about it. The velvet is beautifully smooth, Mr Yates! The carpet never sheds fluff, the doors of the cabinet never squeak. Now I'll never get anything to put behind the glass. Never, never!

Miss Ross had transferred her toadying to Amy since Miss Sheldon left. Miss Ross expressed her loyalty and dedication by being the last of the girls to leave. On two occasions she had brought gifts of oranges from the Rosses' garden with the promise of marmalade when sugar became plentiful after the war. Miss Ross looked up, surprised to see Amy starting to tidy her desk a minute before five o'clock.

Victor lingered back for another reason. He travelled part of the way home with Bonnie, but earned her wrath if he arrived early at the shop and hung about too long waiting for her to close up.

Today Amy ran down the stairs ahead of both, dismissing the idea of taking the train. I will walk if it kills me, she said, nearly crying. Nearing Crystal Street she began to worry about Kathleen. Perhaps she would find her huddled in a heap weeping, perhaps with her things in her case expecting Amy to take her to the train and send her off to Nowra, or perhaps she was already gone.

Amy's throat felt tight, her ankles wobbled, breaking into a run.

But Kathleen was by the side of the house where the concrete path was at its widest, and had it marked out for hopscotch. Crouched down nearby with her tunic hem scraping the ground was a girl about Kathleen's age, intent on watching Kathleen hop with large confident steps from square to square.

Kathleen did not appear to pay much attention to Amy's arrival, except to hook a thick bunch of hair over an ear so that the nearest eye could see more clearly.

The thin little girl with straight black bobbed hair, brown eyes and cheeks dusted with freckles, stood up, biting her bottom lip, too afraid to look into Amy's face.

"I got into a good class," Kathleen said, making a great jump, both legs flying outwards, stretching her dress to its limits.

"Tina knows where I can get my tunic!" Kathleen called to Amy, flinging herself around with a mighty hop. Tina with such credentials felt bold enough to look at Amy's waist.

"We're getting it after school tomorrow!" Kathleen then flopped down on the step with exaggerated sighing and blowing out of her cheeks.

Tina began to hop sedately, a little self-consciously, her black hair flying out like a crow's wing.

"Do you like skipping?" Kathleen called to her. "We can skip here if Amy has a rope!"

122

20

Months later, in bed one night, Amy asked Kathleen if Tina was still her best friend.

"Sort of," Kathleen said. "She's leaving after the Inter." The "Inter" was the Intermediate Certificate which children sat for after three years at high school. They left then for jobs in business and trades if these were available. Others with parents able to afford it and with the mental ability to cope, went on for two more years to take the Leaving Certificate, aiming at professional careers in teaching, medicine, and engineering. Amy never heard reference to careers and examinations without thinking of Peter. Always she had to stifle a notion that efforts like his, resulting only in death, were a waste.

It appeared Kathleen was bent on taking her Leaving Certificate. "Aunty Daph said I could have Peter's books if they still use those at college."

Amy, glimpsing under her closed eyes the years of struggle ahead, felt chilled in the warm bed, which now had an extra blanket.

She had got the blanket through Lance's liaison with woollen mills. A mill had sent him half a dozen left over from an Army order. Two made a wedding present for Victor, one went to Tom Yates, one to Lance and the other to Amy. "It's not the black market you hear about," Amy explained to Kathleen. Their two heads (Amy's and Kathleen's) had bowed for a long time over the blanket, a creamy thing with a little fuzz of beautiful soft wool coating it and a binding in green thread, in what Kathleen told Amy was blanket stitch, top and bottom.

"Tina does it lovely," Kathleen said.

Tina wanted to work somewhere as a seamstress. She couldn't wait to leave school.

"She's mad," Kathleen said, turning over for sleep.

It did not always come so easily for Amy. She was managing from pay to pay, but only now and then was she able to put aside a few shillings apart from money for light and gas. She had to fight her resentment when she looked inside her handbag and saw the flatness of the compartment where she kept her savings.

Since Kathleen had come she had bought nothing for the house, until one Saturday morning when they went to a group of shops, reached by some back streets, where Amy had heard there were bargains in meat and fruit.

They came upon a dark little tavern of a shop with a sullen-eyed man, wearing a heavy overcoat in spite of the warm day, leaning in the doorway. Behind him were piled up goods—strips of carpet, commode cabinets, bed ends, fire tongs, fenders, pictures in heavy frames, kitchen dressers.

The man seemed determined to keep the stock intact. He looked past Amy and Kathleen up the street, a dark shadow on his chin for he had not shaved, then turned and sauntered along the narrow passage between the piles of furniture to disappear.

Amy and Kathleen took a few nervous steps inside and watched for someone to appear. A sign above the door said Quality Fruit and Vegetables, half the first word erased. Obviously the shop had just changed hands and the new owner, anxious to erase its past and promise much better for the future, was working on the old sign between other more pressing duties. Probably, thought Amy, it was the woman coming towards them, small and dark and anxious.

Kathleen's full attention was given to a student's desk astride a wire mattress, like a rider on an emaciated grey horse.

"Look!" Kathleen cried, lifting shining eyes. Pleading and apologetic, she looked at Amy who didn't want to nod but did.

"How much?" Kathleen asked, swinging back her hair.

"Jack!" the woman called to the back. "What do we want for the little table?"

"A desk! Oh, a desk!" Kathleen breathed to Amy, as if she feared it might turn into an ordinary table under their eyes. She stroked a wooden panel and it moved.

"Oh, look!" she cried, for the panel was one that lifted to make more desk space and behind it there were half a dozen little drawers.

125

"Look!" she cried again.

"Jack!" called the woman with her head turned to the back. The answer was a scrape of a cough, then silence and a shout: "Put it down or I'll murder you!" A child cried, and the woman, flashing frightened eyes first to the back then to Amy and Kathleen, told them seven shillings would be alright.

They carried the desk to Crystal Street, taking a longer route by using back streets to avoid crowds. Kathleen's spirits were so high she bounded along, her side of the desk held higher than Amy's. Amy, trying not to think of the mirror or little half table she would have liked for the hall, had to fight back resentment when her handbag, carried awkwardly on an arm, and now almost completely depleted of savings, reminded her of this by slapping into her side.

Kathleen eased the desk to the ground against a high paling fence. "I think I know why that man was so terrible!" she cried. Amy did not want a reason gasped out now. They did not have far to go, only half a dozen houses to pass, then a lane taking them into Crystal Street with a few hundred yards more. If they hurried they would miss three giggling girls coming towards them, arms bound around each other. Kathleen gave them one of her sharp blue stares and a toss of her head, which said they would not in their extreme stupidity have any use for a desk.

The subject of the shopkeeper was not raised until an hour later, after the desk was in place in the bedroom. Amy was pleased too at the way it took care of the empty space along one wall. They were eating their sandwiches of German sausage and tomato sauce, which they attacked with a ravenous hunger after the long walk loaded with the desk and string bag of shopping.

"That man," Kathleen said, dipping her head sideways the way she did when she had something of importance to say. "That man didn't want that shop. It was the woman's idea."

Amy recalled his bowed and sulky shoulders going to the back of the premises and the woman's anxious unhappy face coming forward.

"It would be awful if he got so angry one day he smashed everything up on her.

"I'm glad we got the desk first though." Amy could see that the edges of Kathleen's appetite were sated and she would fly off any moment and set out her books on the desk.

"I'm never getting married myself," she said.

Amy agreed to go out with Lance.

Victor was on his honeymoon and Lance used his office a lot of the time working on accounts and wages. Since Victor had come and the dry cleaning shop opened, normally Lance was not often upstairs. Amy was relieved at this, and glad that Victor and Bonnie were only able to have two weeks' stay at Katoomba in the Blue Mountains following their marriage. She wanted an opportunity to mention to Lance that she was no longer obligated to him in regard to the furniture since sufficient time had passed for her to have worked off the debt.

She watched for her chance and one afternoon, seeing Miss Ross make her way out at last after asking Amy three times if there was anything else to be done, Amy sat on the edge of the chair by Lance's desk. His smile oiled his eyes and she thought it was their colour, with more yellow in the hazel than grey, that gave them their moist look. Amy thought they were not bad eyes though, and if there were no Mrs Lance and she was truly Miss Fowler, she would not mind going out with him. But then if he were free Miss Sheldon would still be around and Amy would not want a contest with her, she reflected, growing a little fearful, as if in some way Miss Sheldon had left her presence behind to watch what was happening.

Amy cleared her throat and Lance made fists of both his hands and rested his chin on them.

"Are you satisfied Mr Yates that the furniture you bought for my house is cut out now?"

Lance appeared to be considering this, looking for and finding some humour in the statement. If he laughs I will die, Amy thought.

There was a ruler by Lance's blotting pad. He picked it up, and reaching across, laid it lightly on Amy's cheek. She blushed and jerked back.

"Why don't you and I go out for dinner? Then we can say the furniture is cut out."

"Oh I couldn't Mr Yates!" Amy was blushing again. "I couldn't! I have my sister living with me now."

She sounded to Lance like a little girl invited into a house to play but unable to because she was minding a baby sister.

Now it was said Amy felt a great relief, as people do when at last they know they are recovering from an illness. She actually put her chin up the way Kathleen did when a challenge was at hand. Amy's smile was for Kathleen although Lance thought it was for him.

She pulled her skirt tightly across her knees. "She's been with me most of the year going to school." Now it didn't seem to matter whether Kathleen was daughter or sister.

They heard Tom's feet on the back stairs and Amy rose quickly, then attempted to disguise the action by leisurely tucking the chair under the desk.

"Alright, Miss Fowler!" Lance said. "Remind me again tomorrow!" He slid his eyes, from which the oil had now drained away, to meet Tom's.

Remind me again tomorrow! Remind me again tomorrow! She beat the words under the soles of her shoes along the darkened pavement. People were coming towards her on their way home, their faces washed white by the lighted windows, then greenish like painted clowns when struck by the lights from cars. None looked happy, or eager to be going home. Remind me again tomorrow! Go to hell, Lance Yates! I won't be reminding you. I'll be keeping out of your way! If taking me out for a meal is so innocent why do you have to dismiss me in front of your brother? I hate your oily skin and your slippery eyes! Don't slip them my way, if you please.

She trembled and breathed hard into a ham and beef shop, the corner of the high counter piercing her breasts until she felt the pain and moved back. The hanging light was bright as a moon, making the shop a cosy shell of a place with the blinds drawn on the front window for the blackout. It turned the window display into a great bountiful larder of grey-skinned fowls, pink Devon sausage, piled orange-skinned saveloys, rounds of cheese, pickled onions, rows of meat pies, trays of cakes, some with yellow custard between slabs of pastry, and another kind consisting of a black mess of cake and currants and raisins between pastry too. The latter were called Chester cakes. Kathleen loved them. Amy asked for two and two pieces of the fowl, trembling in its gelatine and parsley petticoat. She would warm it over a saucepan of hot water, and boil potatoes and a wedge of cabbage from the garden. She had to swallow away her hunger and resist clawing inside the paper bag for some chicken skin.

Kathleen was in the bedroom at her desk, copying from a text book into an exercise book. She had left the light on in the kitchen.

"Two lights, Kathleen, when you're only using one!" Amy cried, coming down the hall. Kathleen sprang from her seat and stood in sentry pose holding the cord that controlled the bedroom light, switching it off the moment Amy had shed her coat and put her bag away. Then she hooped an arm around Amy's waist and kept in step with her to the kitchen, laughing and throwing her young leg against Amy's thigh.

"Oh, get off!" Amy cried, laughing too. "And let me get the tea!"

Next morning at Lincolns there was a sealed envelope with Amy's name on it under the cover of her typewriter. She read it on her lap. *Dear Miss Fowler* (the note said) *I meant it about making a little occasion of ending the furniture agreement with dinner as my guest.*

There was a good space after the last word, as if Lance was considering adding another sentence. *Bring your sister*, he had written.

Amy stuffed the note back in its envelope and put it in her handbag with her savings, little as they were, but the letter seemed to make them more. Yes, I'll keep that, she said to herself, smoothing it out against the side of the compartment. My goodness me, I feel I own not only the furniture but the whole of Sydney! Her typewriter rattled so hard Miss Ross felt quite despondent. She would never match that.

At tea in the Petersham kitchen Amy waited for her chance to tell Kathleen about the dinner. Amy was coming home at the normal time the following Friday evening and they were both to be dressed for Lance to pick them up and take them to Romano's, a high-class restaurant where important people dined and sometimes got their pictures in the newspapers. Amy stole frequent looks at Kathleen's face, nursing the secret, anticipating the joy of revealing it.

Kathleen shook the tablecloth free of crumbs and put it back for breakfast with the salt and pepper shakers in the centre, alongside the cruet and sugar bowl. She felt a sense of pleasure when this was done. At home in Diggers Creek, the table was used after meals for May's ironing, Gus's farm catalogues, spread out to get the best of the lamplight, and sometimes a game of cards, played with a greasy pack until Norman and Fred yawned away to bed to read paperback novels about ranch life in America, and dream of girls.

"Doing anything with Tina this weekend?" Amy asked.

Kathleen sometimes spent Saturday afternoon at Tina's place. Tina's mother was Greek, and allowed Tina and Kathleen to help make cabbage rolls and slabs of sweets and eat some on upturned boxes in the backyard. Tina's father, Greek too, was a partner in a fruit and vegetable shop and brought the boxes home with the bottoms covered with speckled fruit which the family ate, after which they turned the boxes into firewood.

Other times she went to Coxes with Amy, and once or twice she had been taken along in the truck John now owned for a short ride somewhere, mostly with Helen, the girl next door, as well, for she and John were courting seriously now. Amy was saddened by this. John changed towards me, she thought, from the time I got the furniture, or it might have been Kathleen coming. This amused her a little, for John, a bit slow mentally, might not have quite believed Amy had children until he saw Kathleen.

Amy gave the window ledges a good wipe with the dishcloth, then hung it on the little wire line John had fixed to the corner between stove and window.

"John used to be always doing little things for me," she murmured, putting off the pleasure of the announcement about the dinner still further.

"That was BH," said Kathleen.

"BH?" Amy wrinkled her nose and forehead towards the ceiling.

"Before Helen!" Kathleen swung the tea-towel like a stockwhip then stretched it across another line John had attached to the wall.

"Oh, you're crazy!" Amy cried, loving her for it.

The kitchen was neat, Amy had made out her shopping list for Saturday morning and propped it against the tea caddy on the mantlepiece, turning it to a different angle to invite Kathleen's comment on such advanced attention to this small chore, but none was forthcoming.

"Come and we'll sit in the sitting room and talk about what we'll do!" Amy said, leading the way.

"I should take my *King Lear*, I suppose," Kathleen said.

"Oh, bother that old has-been! Let's live for tomorrow!" Amy was a little jealous of Kathleen's familiarity with Shakespeare. She had only learned the Seven Ages of Man in sixth class at Diggers Creek.

Kathleen sprawled on a chair and Amy wedged herself into the corner of the lounge, and after a moment reached down for the sewing, which was rolled up and tucked under a cushion.

"That's where I'll put *King Lear* next time!" Kathleen cried. "Cheat!"

Amy had made a blouse on Daphne's machine, and was now doing the buttonholes and sewing on small pearl buttons. She would wear it to the dinner. It's worked out so well, Amy thought, Kathleen coming. I wouldn't like it on my own, and I don't even need to remind her that we are supposed to be sisters, for it seems we really are.

She bit off a thread of cotton, slipped it into the eye of her needle and held her work close to her face to make the first stitches.

"In case I haven't mentioned it already," Amy said, "tomorrow night you and I are dining out!"

"Whoopee!" Kathleen yelled and flung her feet to the floor and whirled in a dance, an old pleated skirt of Amy's flying out around her.

She had few clothes, keeping her schoolwear in meticulous order, and looking out for letters from Fred, now in the Northern Territory, who often sent a pound note, which

134

Kathleen usually spent on such things as shorts for school sports, or an extra blouse.

"Oh, goody!" she would cry, kissing it before waving it above her head. Amy was pleased too, Kathleen managed the money carefully, although Amy felt disappointed that she seldom shared any small luxury item with her, like a chocolate bar or ice-cream cone. She sees me as the provider, and I suppose she is right, Amy decided.

"Now sit down in ladylike fashion," Amy said, stitching with great care. "And listen while I tell you."

"Certainly, Granma!" Kathleen cried, with straight back and straight face and arms folded. She moved them down below the ridge of her breasts and Amy slipped the point of her needle into her skin and flung the blouse away to save it from a bloody stain.

"Oh, watch out!" she cried. Watch out, I'm sounding like a grandmother! Watch out, she's growing up too fast with those breasts! Amy sucked her finger silently.

After it was safe to stitch again she said: "My boss Mr Yates is taking us both to dinner in a posh restaurant."

"Mr Yates! I've never met him. Is he a married man?"

"Of course he's a married man!" Amy said. "He has a son a bit older than you."

"Keep him away then. I don't like goony boys!"

"The boy is not coming," Amy said.

"Is the wife?" Kathleen asked.

Amy studied the buttonhole smoothed out on her knee. "It's not that sort of an evening out. It's a kind of thank you to me for extra work." She looked down on the lounge seat as if it might speak in support of this.

"Oh," Kathleen said, with her mouth shaped like the letter similarly named.

There was silence while Amy put her pink face close to her sewing.

"He's not doing a line for you, is he?" Kathleen asked.

"Of course he's not doing a line for me! He's asking you too."

"Very nice of him! Very nice indeed!" Kathleen slumped back in her chair, hooked a leg over the arm and swung it.

"You can wear your brown dress," Amy said. "We'll be warm in the car."

The brown dress, also made on Daphne's machine, was of cinnamon-coloured wool with a lace collar and cuffs, a row of buttons from neck to waist covered with the material, and a belt drawing in Kathleen's slender waist.

For several moments Kathleen knocked a heel against the side of her chair.

"What will you wear?" she asked, so abruptly that Amy felt slapped. She folded the blouse with great care, sleeve to sleeve, Kathleen watching.

You're wearing that, said the accusing eyes. You made it especially for going out with him.

She got up and left the room and Amy watched the door almost in disbelief. In a little while she came back with *King Lear*.

Amy went to Brennans in Newtown in her lunch hour next day and bought two pairs of silk stockings at three and elevenpence each. It is stupid the way I am sucking up to her, Amy thought, but all the time imagining handing the stockings to Kathleen when she got home to Petersham.

Kathleen had never had silk stockings, and if Amy hadn't become friendly with a girl in underwear and hosiery she would never have been allowed two pairs. Silk stockings had all but disappeared with wartime rationing. A dye to paint legs was hailed with great enthusiasm until it was discovered that perspiring feet sent the dye running into shoes and it was abandoned. Legs were bared, except in the event of gifts of stockings from American servicemen, repaying households for their hospitality during Rest and Recreation leave.

Good-looking girls crossing long silken legs in trams and trains were given long hard stares and it was whispered more than once: "A Yank's ground sheet, bet your money on that!"

The stockings quivered from their wrapping, shimmering as they dropped fold after fold from Kathleen's hands. She was on a chair in the sitting room, ready in her brown dress. She whipped off her white socks with one hand and drew the stockings on up to her thighs, after a moment raising agonized eyes to Amy.

"Garters!" she cried. Amy ran for her chocolate box of cottons where a roll of elastic and scissors was tucked into a corner.

"Good and beautiful Amy!" Kathleen cried, throwing out a leg to bind the elastic around her thigh, snip the length off, then begin a matching one, moistening the end of the cotton with a dart of her little tongue before threading the needle.

Amy went to the bedroom and sat on the bed and closed her eyes. "Thank heavens," she said aloud. "Thank, thank heavens!" She caught up her blouse and ran to the kitchen to heat the iron.

Amy had to restrain Kathleen from opening the front door and waiting in the doorway or on the step.

"In the sitting room! We'll wait there," she said, brushing her skirt, although it was spotless, newly dry cleaned at Lincoln's shop.

"I know why that place is called Maytime Dry Cleaning," Kathleen said.

"Of course. Because May is a nice fresh white flower," Amy answered.

"No!" And Kathleen's hair swung back and forth like a branch in a gale. "It's the letters of your name."

"Oh, rubbish!" Amy said.

"You've gone red."

"I have not!" Amy spoke too soon, before she opened her little powder compact and studied her face.

The doorbell rang and Amy's body jerked and Kathleen raised a cool hand. "The reason I'm going tonight is to watch out for you, Amy."

She slipped past her to open the door, speaking over her shoulder with her hand on the knob. "Someone has to."

Amy was so quiet throughout the dinner that Lance gave up after a while and concentrated on Kathleen.

"What do you do at school?" Lance asked, digging his spoon into his lemon souffle, wondering if it might sweeten Amy up. She was sitting there very stiff about the face, not eating with the gusto he expected. Having sneaked a look at her occasionally at Lincolns, tucking into what looked like ordinary sandwiches, he had looked forward to watching her at work on something more exotic. He rather hoped to see a childish bulge in her cheeks, gone very pink both with pleasure and embarrassment at the show of greed.

Here she was, eating with ladylike bites, tipping half back on her plate from each forkful and taking the food between her teeth as if she didn't want her lips to go near it.

Lance felt the evening was so far a failure, and that to save it he had better turn his attention to Kathleen, the sister. She was a pretty little thing, older looking than a schoolgirl, more of the elder sister look he thought, seeing her eyes flash from Amy's plate to Amy's face from time to time.

Kathleen emptied her mouth, dabbed it with her serviette and swept her hair away in her effort to give her attention to Lance's question.

"We do all the subjects. Biology I like. It would be wonderful to be a doctor."

Lance straightened with respect. Amy straightened too, but to avoid a slump of neck and shoulders. It was going to be an effort to finish her souffle.

"I got a boy your age, a bit older," he said, thinking of Allan in a white coat. He was getting on better with his son now. Allan had grown taller, lost some of his pimples and his fat and wasn't hanging around his mother so much.

Lance began to think of an outing—himself, Allan, Amy and this girl—on one of the Sundays Eileen spent with her parents, who hung on in their old house in Lewisham. Eileen went there as often as she could to cook, clean and wash for the old pair, sighing a good deal of the time and making frequent reference to the selfishness of other members of the family, who left the task almost entirely to her. She would probably be glad to be dropped off and then Lance could wheel the car around and go back for Amy and Kathleen. If the boy was with them, Eileen would see no harm in it. Better still he could make an excuse of seeing to something at Lincolns, taking the boy with him. He glanced at Amy taking little sips of her coffee. She might be happier on a picnic, sitting on the grass near a spread tablecloth with the breeze blowing about her fair hair. Maybe crowds of people upset her.

On the other hand they did not seem to upset the younger one. She screwed her head around to watch the dancers on a square of floorboards fitted into the carpet. The space was not much bigger than the supper table in the Diggers Creek hall, Kathleen was thinking.

"Would you like a dance?" Lance said before he quite knew he had said it.

Kathleen stood at once and tucked her chair under the table. Lance liked that. She didn't protest about being unable to dance, or hang her head and go red. He looked swiftly at Amy, thinking that was what she might have done. Amy got up a small smile, and Lance thought she might be glad to have the table to herself for a while. He stood quickly as if this was the message he received from her, and went quite eagerly to slip an arm around Kathleen and lead her onto the floor. She put her head back and lowered her eyelids, and laid the tips of her fingers in Lance's palm.

"We have dancing once a week at school," she murmured. "I am the boy mostly. It's good to be the girl."

It was a foxtrot and to Lance's surprise Kathleen danced it well. When he paused and crossed his feet and made his body crooked, she ran with her feet slipping in and out in tiny steps to get close to his, not looking down, although people at the tables were.

She was nearly as tall as he was, and he thought he had never had a moment in all his life like this. She was soft and light as a bird, her brown dress birds' feathers he needed to press into to find her body. It quivered but not

with fear. This light and lovely creature, scented faintly
with boronia, he thought, but more with flesh, warm and
neutral. He thought if she were stripped of her clothes, her
body would be a paler brown, a creamy gold, deeper than
the collar of her dress. He closed his eyes a moment and
felt his hand was on the skin of her waist, smooth as the
skin of her palm now curled inside his other hand, softer
though, more flesh to dig into and spring back, not like the
doughy flesh of older women, and he thought with shame of
Eileen, whose waist had never been firm, and she didn't like
it grasped anyway, and kept her nightdress there in folds,
never allowing it hitched higher and often folding her arms
on her breasts to keep his hands from them.

This girl, this angel, would be shy, but proud of her
body, opening her arms to him, lighting the darkness like
a flame.

He took her back to the table and was surprised to see
Amy there.

143

There was no picnic, no meeting with the Yates boy, no possibility of Lance viewing the naked body of Kathleen.

Amy gave Lance her notice, even without another job.

After the dinner she barely spoke to Kathleen and Kathleen gave a show of barely noticing. She went off soberly to school a little earlier than before, saying goodbye to the knob as she opened the door. She crossed the street to Tina's house to wait for her there. Before, it was mostly Tina who came to wait for Kathleen.

Even Tina noticed Amy's mood.

"Jings she's crabby," she said to Kathleen a few days later as they walked close to the paling fence, taking the short cut to school.

Kathleen stopped, swinging around, lifting her chin, lowering her eyes.

"If you can keep a secret I will tell you," she said. Other groups of girls jerked past, knees lifted, their tunics playing the pleats, cases clanging against cases, bursts of laughter, a shriek or two, like hurrying navy blue sheep given voices.

Kathleen waited until they were well ahead. "Both of us are in love with the same man!" She kept her eyes closed, only opening them when there was the bite of Tina's fingers into her forearm.

She flew ahead, calling back, "I'll race you!" She didn't stop until she was panting along the school veranda, met there by Miss Parks who said with indulgence: "Not so fast, Kathleen! Ladies don't gallop."

Miss Parks gave Tina the smallest and coolest of nods, a pupil with lesser academic potential warranting no more; whereas Kathleen was one of the school's brightest students. Miss Parks had her for English and loved her quickness, so many others were intelligent but dreamy. She felt a rising excitement watching her work, throwing that hair around to get it out of the way, face tilted sideways over her essay.

Miss Parks often wondered what would become of her. Dear Lord, she prayed, not a housewife in a dirty little place surrounded by grubby children, and a wet-lipped man with hairs all over his chest coming home the worse for drink.

Miss Parks, aged thirty-eight, shuddered, but felt a creeping of her loins holding the thought to her, transferred to the rub of hairs against her own naked thighs. Nonsense, nonsense! She belonged to a family of eight and saw her sisters, pretty and clever, go this way. But never

145

her. She went to teachers' college, then to university on scholarships. She had been teaching now for sixteen years, and had a good bank account for her retirement. Twenty years on she would go abroad, walk the halls of Oxford, see Edinburgh, France and Sweden, perhaps murmur to scholars like herself, Yes, I was a teacher in a big girls' school. The musty smells of dusty corridors and books were sweeter than the fumes from the Chelsea Flower Show or the perfume factories of Grasse.

Miss Parks dreamed on of taking Kathleen abroad with her, Kathleen a teacher in some big university, Miss Parks the chaperone and mother figure to the lovely Miss Fowler, who was wed to her career as Miss Parks had been to hers.

Miss Parks changed the course of the rush of love in her loins to the slender shape of Miss Fowler. They'd be Parky and Chook to each other, sharing literary discussions and tea and French pastries in a small but elegant flat furnished in exquisite taste. Together, they would observe the crowds on the Left Bank, take long walks, go to the theatre and art exhibitions and talk into the early morning in their shared bedroom.

When Amy went to work on the Monday after the dinner she watched for Lance to appear. She would greet him a shade more warmly she decided, send a little message of thanks with her eyes for the dinner.

He usually said Good morning, girls! to the office in general, then Good morning, Miss Fowler! sometimes with an excuse to linger at her desk.

This morning he rushed through with a Good morning, all! and went to Victor's office. Victor was back from his honeymoon, even paler of complexion, due to the misty mountain air, disappointed that Bonnie did not care for long walks, but showed a fondness for the home-made chocolates a village cafe was famous for, and for flirting with the hotel owner who did not disguise his fondness for plump little girls with china blue eyes.

Victor bore it all stoically, looking to the time when Bonnie would be installed in their flat, the upper floor of an old stone house in Ashfield, in a frilly apron, and flicking a feather duster over their new furniture.

Bonnie's old boss in the machinery shop did not replace her. He saved on wages by handling the few customers himself. Reading the war news he was fairly confident it would soon end in Europe and the Japanese would be run to ground shortly afterwards.

He had a stout wife with a lot of greying hair wound in plaits who looked foreign, like a German. He brought her into the shop two or three times a week while he went around the import agents, mainly to keep contact with them, for little new stock was coming into the country and even less was being manufactured for anything other than to help win the war.

He was nervous about Freda who hated the Germans as much as he did, but he was afraid anyone coming into the shop might take her for one. She would have been so hurt if he had told her this, or suggested she change her hair style, she would have cried for a week. He just watched people's expressions nervously when he was there with her, and got her to talk so they would know by her accent she was Australian.

Lance made a great show of welcoming Victor back, shaking hands and wrenching at his shoulder, making Victor's face light up, glad the miserable honeymoon was over, and feeling hopeful now that he was back at work, back into the old routine, that he and Bonnie would settle into contented married life, despite her show of impatience and restlessness.

Amy was certain Lance was keeping his back to her intentionally. Her cheeks burned a deep pink. The eyebrows of Miss Ross were raised above her typewriter carriage as she piously rolled paper into her machine.

Amy decided to look for something in her handbag, and seeing the compartment with Lance's note inside about the furniture she gave it a little pinch for reassurance. I am being silly, she thought. He has not changed towards me at all.

"You do these, Miss Ross!" Lance said, coming out of Victor's office with a sheaf of letters. "The replies are written on the back. File them with your carbon copy."

He put a paper weight on them with quite a flourish and darted out.

Amy heard the clang of metal as the drawer of a filing cabinet shot home. "Ouch!" said Miss Armstrong who bruised her fingers. Watching Amy, she had neglected to get them out of the way.

In the days following, Amy hardly glimpsed Lance except to meet him on the front stairs, on her way to the park to eat her lunchtime sandwiches.

148

"Good morning!" Lance said although it was past midday. He went faster up the stairs and Amy went slower down them.

Lance had given Victor his rise in salary. Tom didn't think he should have it. Tom's wife Sadie was talking of sending their eldest girl to boarding school to allow her greater attention to her music. Anything extra the firm could afford would be useful for that.

Lance had felt miserable instead of pleased when Victor, thanking him for the extra pound in his pay packet, said it would take care of the weekly repayments on his furniture. Lance didn't want to be reminded of Amy's furniture. He had acted (he told himself) on an impulse, wanting nothing more than to cheer her drab life, and the same went for taking the two of them out to dinner.

That night Allan had been playing a minor role in a school concert. Lance had said he couldn't be there, he needed to catch up on some work at the office before Victor's return. There was no risk of the lie reaching Randwick. Sadie and Eileen were not speaking, so neither family encroached upon the private life of the other.

The rift started years earlier when Allan ruined a birthday party for Sadie's and Tom's little Jean. Allan swept a knife blade of cream from the top of a sponge cake and aimed it with commendable accuracy at Jean's forehead.

Jean shrieked and smeared her cheek and new party dress with a handful of the cream. The small guests shrieked too for this was more entertaining than Pin the Tail on the Donkey. Sadie shrieked at Eileen when she failed to chastise

Allan, who had whispered to his mother the name Jean called him in reference to his chubby bottom. Eileen with a fat father and two fat brothers felt the humiliation just as deeply.

After the party both women sat by their telephones waiting for an apology from each other. In the end Sadie rang demanding it and Eileen slammed the earpiece so violently into its hook the wall shook, wobbling a picture of the fat father beside it.

After the concert Lance failed to attend, Allan at breakfast next morning bowed mournfully over his plate.

"I'll be there next time," Lance said. Inside himself he was saying how glad he felt to be done with all foolishness, in the next minute bringing a blush to Eileen's cheek with his praise for the crispness of the bacon.

Near the end of the week Amy looked for and found a reason to go downstairs to the factory.

I'll tell him. Now I'll tell him. Her brain tapped out the words. Only her tapping heels spoke them.

The top of Lance's head was visible, bowed between the long cutting-out tables where a hand-operated electric cutter was moving through several thicknesses of fabric. With great concentration, Lance watched the hand of the woman guiding the cutter and gave a little slap of approval to the pile of tunic sleeves she had pushed to one side. He needed to raise his eyes, Amy was so close. She saw them dried of their oil. She plucked a pile of invoices from a spike on a rough little table and ran for the stairs. I hate him, I do, I do. I hate him! So said the soles of her shoes, sluggish on the wood. A great sigh from the presser was in her ears.

That evening over tea in the kitchen, Kathleen broke the silence by asking for money for things from the chemist's for experiments in the school laboratory.

"That's ridiculous!" Amy said. "You're not going to be a chemist!"

"Miss Parks said I could be," Kathleen answered. "But she wants me to be an English teacher."

Amy swept her plate to the bench where the washing up was done.

"I'm giving up my job at Lincolns," Amy said, filling the kettle, the rush of water causing her to raise her voice, the better for her ears to believe it too.

"Good on you, Amy!" Kathleen cried. Amy turned her face in astonishment and Kathleen took the last slice of bread and buttered it with great speed.

Just look at her, Amy thought. Not a care in the world where the next slice is coming from.

"What's so good about it?" Amy asked, taking things from the table speedily too. "Jobs don't grow on trees, you know."

Kathleen chewed and swallowed. "You're very capable, Amy," she said with her eyes on the little line John had put up for the dishcloth. Amy took the cloth and the line slapped the wall a couple of times.

"What did he say when you told him?" Kathleen asked.

Amy pointed her chin at the middle of the window and swirled the soap in its wire holder so hard an angry sea of foam swished against the sides of the dish.

"He simply said I was to train Miss Ross to do my job before I go," she said.

151

"Train Miss Ross to do your job. She's quite able to handle it!" Lance said to Amy when she gave her fortnight's notice.

It was, it had to be, the result of the changes in Lance's life. Allan had started to sing in the Baptist Church Choir. Lance had gone with Eileen to hear him. He had never attended church with Eileen since they were married. He was proud of his son, in his good clothes, his hair done so nicely with just the right amount of hair cream. Eileen with too much scent on was doing all the right things throughout the service. She nudged him when he did not appear to be going to rise with the congregation. He was daydreaming. That was his boy up there, better looking than the others, a bright lad who would take over Lincolns one day. He would join Lance there in what time? Three, four years at the most. Almost tomorrow! My God it was closer than he thought.

Eileen heard his breath go out in a puff, like someone blowing at a dandelion. She looked in his face and got a reassuring slide of his eyes in return. She shut her own on her rouged cheeks to pray on and Lance prayed too. He hardly knew what to say but keeping his eyes squeezed shut he got started. I love that boy up there and if you can help me take good care of him, get him into Lincolns when he's old enough, I'll do a few things around the church as Eileen has always wanted, fixing the windows (he opened his eyes to check them and could not see anything wrong although she complained about the way they rattled in windy weather), anything at all, cleaning the grounds with the other men (Eileen did all the gardening at home), I will do anything you ask if that boy will love me back. I think he will. And looking earnestly at the singing group, Lance felt sure Allan quirked an eyebrow of recognition over the top of his music sheet.

Faith of our Far-ar-thers, living still, in spite of dungeon, fire and sword! The words were almost shouted down on the heads of the congregation, some tilted upwards, Lance's in particular, mesmerized by his son's open mouth, the skin stretched on his jaws, even his eyes were singing. Faith! Lance felt it wash over him as strong as the sound. By heavens yes, he would have faith!

God had given him a son years before Tom. (Thank You!) Allan would be well installed long before Tom's boy would be ready (if he ever was) to come into the business. Lance saw the two of them, himself and Allan, talking on their way to work and home, business of course. The boy would learn everything. "This is my son," he would say to colleagues, proud of him in his suit and tie. He would learn to run the office too. Victor or no Victor, the place (after the war) would be big enough for them all. The war! Please God it would be over before Allan was old enough to go. (There was good reason for praying there!) His boy dying like that cousin of little Miss Fowler's! Up there alive and strong and beautiful. Lance felt the moisture on his face and turned his thoughts to the Fowler girls for distraction.

He did a foolish thing with that furniture and dinner, but he would put it well behind him. With Allan around there would be no indiscretions, no entanglements, he would make sure of that. You never knew with people like the Fowlers. That talk of the young one becoming a doctor could be all ballyhoo. Most likely she would leave school and want a job at Lincolns. From tomorrow he would be a model of discretion, someone a son could be proud of. To think at that dinner he actually thought of Allan and that girl...! Lead me not into temptation (he knew that part of the prayer well enough!).

The congregation was standing. Lance opened his mouth and pushed a finger and thumb into each corner looking at Eileen. She took a handkerchief and wiped at the lipstick trickled there and asked with her eyes if that was right. Lance's eyes replied yes and he pressed back in the pew to let her pass. He even touched her doughy waist on the way out.

It was nothing short of a miracle the way it happened, Miss Fowler lifting her face to say something when he was on his way to Victor's office, and Lance hurrying past

154

keeping his eyes on Victor's door. Not the time and place for conversation thank you all the same, said his back, giving a little shake in its grey suit striped with a deeper grey, the zigzag pattern sending a quiver across Lance's shoulders like a sudden chill wind across water.

The Misses Ross, Armstrong, Harris and the new junior all saw. A little burning of their cheeks said this would breathe life into the lunch hour, thank heavens only thirty minutes off.

Amy rose and went into Victor's office. Both men heard the scrape of chair legs and turned surprised, quite hostile eyes, petulance there too. Who does she think she is interrupting this way?

"I'd like to mention to you, Mr Yates, that I am leaving here in two weeks. I'll want a reference too for my new job."

She trembled for a long time when she was back at her desk but no one noticed.

I started here with a lie, and ended the same way, Amy thought. But never mind.

When Kathleen was a few weeks from her seventeenth birthday she folded her arms across her breasts, flicked her hair from her face as was her habit and told Amy her plans.

They were in the Petersham kitchen. It looked different, so did Amy, and Amy, throwing her hands up to press her cheeks, kept her eyes from Kathleen, too afraid to face the difference there.

"But I bought you a single bed!" she cried, foolishly she knew, but it was the first thing to fly into her mind.

The incident of the single bed had happened years earlier in the week that Amy gave Lance Yates her notice.

Amy and Kathleen were in bed, Kathleen taller and a little heavier than Amy, her well-shaped bust straining her old nightdress, the strain of their relationship since the dinner with Lance causing each to jerk away when flesh touched flesh.

"When you get your new job, Amy, I'd like a bed of my own," Kathleen said quite amiably. "I've already got my pillow."

Daphne had given her a spare pillow she had as soon as she saw the pillowcase stuffed with a sheet that Kathleen used for several weeks after she came to Sydney.

Amy's body turned with such a violent movement the bedclothes were pulled from Kathleen, who pulled them back just as violently.

"See what I mean?" she cried.

"See what *you* mean!" Amy shouted the first part of the sentence, the last part a squeak for there was a cough from one of the Misses Wheatley above the ceiling.

"And that's another thing," Kathleen said, swooping foward, rearranging the bedclothes on them both, then sliding carefully back onto her pillow to keep them in place. "Those Wheatley women should be asked to leave."

"Those Wheatley women, I'll have you know, keep a roof over our heads!"

There was another cough from overhead and Kathleen answered with a loud artificial cough of her own, which caused Amy to say "Shush, shush!" in a hoarse whisper.

"Calm yourself down, Amy," Kathleen said. "I only want what's best for you."

"You want what's best for me. I like that!" All I can do, Amy thought, is repeat her words. I haven't any conversation of my own any more.

Kathleen was back on her pillow, very calm. "So far you've done a very good thing getting away from that Lincoln man."

Amy was about to shriek: "So I've done a very good thing, have I?" then stopped herself. She crunched the blankets under her chin, while Kathleen smoothed the sheet back to free her own.

"The man is married, and would use you for his own ends. I see that very plainly." Kathleen was still using her amiable, even pleasant tone.

"I can't stand the greasy-skinned thing, I'm always telling you!"

"People in love always say that."

"In love! What would you know about it?"

There was a small silence before Kathleen answered. "There is this boy I like."

Amy listened. Kathleen's voice was a kind she had never heard before. She thought of rain falling on a tree, sending the leaves brushing against each other making a whispery sound, a light and slithery noise, so gentle it was hardly audible. Hardly a noise at all, a precious sound, thin but strong, only ears trained hard would hear the vibrancy. Only the whispering, rustling noise telling of the rain, so light you would not know it was falling at all sheltered by the tree.

"We walk home from school together. Tina goes ahead."

"Very obliging of her!" Amy made a show of wanting sleep, turning over to be ready for it.

What was this boy like? A succession of boys' faces raced before Amy's shut eyes, pasty, pimply pale, round eyes that said nothing, mouths falling open. Peter's face came up after a while, smooth and golden, the lips raised just enough to show the tips of his white teeth, his blue eyes crinkled like water with the sun and a breeze teasing it.

Amy opened her eyes. "How long have you known this boy?"

"Since Monday."

Amy pushed her body deeper into the bed, wriggled once and was still. In a moment Kathleen slipped from her side and taking her pillow wrapped in her arms went to stand by the window.

"You'll freeze to death!" Amy cried. Kathleen's shape was in silhouette against the street light. The pillow was held so that a bulge of it rested on Kathleen's stomach.

"Come back to bed!" Amy shouted, mainly to cover the fear in her voice, but she doubted Kathleen would detect it, there with a cheek laid on the pillow end.

Amy climbed from the bed and grabbing a coat from a chairback laid it across Kathleen's shoulders. Her arms stayed along the shoulders.

Kathleen laid her face on Amy's neck and, when the coat fell to the floor, still wrapped in the embrace they went back to bed.

Amy got a job in materials at Anthony Horderns.

She honoured her promise to Kathleen, and taking advantage of a discount for employees bought a single bed and mattress from her first pay. Kathleen, almost hysterical with joy, helped her set it up in the small room opposite the one she shared with Amy, closed until now. Kathleen dragged her desk in too and Amy noticed she did not treat it as reverently as she had when they carried it home from the shop.

"I wonder is that shop still there with the same man and woman," Amy murmured.

Kathleen, dumping books in careless fashion on the desk top, seemed not to have heard. She was anxious to make up the bed and when she smoothed the blanket out, the one they got while Amy was at Lincolns, she thanked Amy yet again for allowing her to have it.

"Old Greasy Guts was a bit handy at times, wasn't he?

"You know what I think I'll do, Amy? I'll ask Tina to show me how to crochet and I'll make a cover, in a pale colour like green so that the blanket will show through it." She stood back, hands on hips, head to one side.

"Have you homework for Monday?" Amy asked. The books on the desk had an abandoned air and Amy went and made them neat.

"Oh, I'll waltz through that old exam, never fear, Amy dear!"

"And the old exam after that, the one for your Leaving Certificate?"

"I may as well tell you," Kathleen said, her eyes lingering on the bed, admiring the pillow in a freshly laundered slip, the corners stiff and shining with starch, looking sharp enough to cut.

"And I'll crochet a sham for the pillow as well, Amy!" And Kathleen in her delight jumped backwards to sit on her desk and swing her legs vigorously over the edge.

Amy, wanting to sit down but not prepared to use the bed, waited, her folded arms squashing her breasts.

"I'm leaving after the Inter, Amy. That's fair warning."

Amy turned to the bed and turned the pillow to its other side, needing to reverse it at once, for on that side it exposed one of Amy's beautiful little darns on the slip.

"You're staying at school. Of course you are!"

"Of course I'm not, Amy! Now be a sensible girl and listen to reason."

"Only two more years is reason enough to stay on!"

Kathleen waggled her head, but her hair did not swing with the vibrancy of the old days. It was grown-up hair now, cut below her ears. Kathleen put her hands to it and turned the ends under in the pageboy style not allowed for schooldays. She looked for a mirror, but the little cane dressing-table was in the other room.

"I need to get a mirror and something to hang my clothes in," she said, frowning at the space along the walls.

Amy left for the kitchen. Now ride this out with calmness, she told herself. She has no intention of leaving school! To help stifle her fears she swung chairs onto the table and caught up the broom to give the floor its thorough weekly sweep. I will think about my job, she decided, with a lift in spirits.

She was glad to have the counter to herself, wartime rationing was still in force and one salesgirl was considered enough for the section. The sharp, slightly acid smell of the new materials when the paper was torn from them was pleasing to Amy and had the effect of taking the edge off the strangeness she felt in new surroundings.

She arranged the bolts of material to give the illusion of full shelves and stood some of the more brightly patterned rolls on their ends on the counter, loosening the last few folds to have them fall in a drape as if a provocative knee was thrust out behind.

The floorwalker saw and bowed towards it. He was always bowing. He bowed to customers and to heads of the company visiting the floor, though never to the staff below him, and had Amy known it, the honour of having her work bowed to was great indeed. He was very pale of eye with a skin not unlike a piece of creased unbleached calico. The top of his head was quite bald, and he attempted to disguise this by parting his hair low on one side and spreading the strands across to the other. Amy was intrigued by this and had to check her stare. Why did he do it, she wondered. It only made his baldness more of a baldness. Hey there, she said to herself, making a neat pile of the pattern books for customers to choose styles, I'm back to finding odd things about faces! Now there's a good sign.

But bending down to make her personal things neat on the shelf under the counter, there was the intrusion of Lance's face. His yellowy eyes were soft the way she saw them at Lincolns when they trailed with tender amusement over her comb and soap and little mirror under the counter there.

Briskly she began rerolling a bolt of cream flannelette for babies' layettes. I know what I'll do, she decided, I'll measure up all the short rolls and mark them so that I'll know how much is there when a customer asks, and I won't waste time on measuring.

The floorwalker, Mr Benson, came up and watched her write twelve yards and four inches in the tiniest figures in the world on a selvedge.

"Only on the shorter rolls to save disappointment if the customer wants more," Amy explained, thinking perhaps she should have asked permission first.

Mr Benson bowed at the figures then walked off thinking he hadn't approved of married women working, but in the case of Mrs Fowler she was a credit to the floor.

In fact Amy, to improve her chances of employment, had said Ted was missing in the war.

"He could be though," Kathleen said. "You could be telling the truth, Amy."

Witnessing the bullying of women in Tina's home by Tina's father and the ill humour of her Uncle Dudley, Kathleen decided she was better off without a father. She often thought fondly of Gus though and wondered if he missed her, since she thought of herself as his favourite. Had he transferred all his affection to Patricia and Lebby?

Gus is probably one of the few decent men in the world, Kathleen thought, reflecting on the few males of her acquaintance. She decided John was not too bad except for his habit of ignoring her when Helen was around. Against such competition, old Greasy Guts did not fare all that badly.

Men, men, oh, mysterious men! she sang to herself, thinking perhaps she could be a songwriter and make that the opening line, then giving the thought away in the distraction of a little pleasing shudder that ran from her knees to her neck.

Amy finished sweeping and made a clatter putting the furniture back in place, and thought about going to Coxes before tea. Daphne would support her on the subject of Kathleen staying at school.

"Kathleen!" she called. "I need another pair of hands out here!" There was no reply and Amy, now in the front room dusting around the windows, switched her thoughts to the curtains she could now buy from furnishings in the store, cheap because of the discount, and felt so cheered she did not call Kathleen again, but went to the back fence for some jonquils that had sprung up there. She put them in her spare jug on the mantlepiece, her head cocked to one side in admiration as she backed out the door.

"Kathleen!" she called along the silent hall. "We'll go to Aunty Daph's. She'll want to hear about my new job!" That was clever of me, she thought.

She went rapidly to look into Kathleen's room. Her clothes, the skirt that was Amy's, the first blouse and jumper she had for school and her bloomers and singlet were piled on the desk.

Kathleen was in bed, one naked shoulder lifted, one naked arm, cream like the creamy blanket lying across it, the points of the pillowcase making slits in her dark hair. Her eyes were closed, her chin was pointed upwards.

Amy, disbelieving, pulled the blanket back to see that all of Kathleen's body was naked between the sheets. She covered her quickly, stepping back red-faced, anger covering her fright.

"That's the silliest sight I've ever seen!"

Kathleen kept her eyes closed. "The human body should never be called silly, Amy."

"What on earth possessed you?—Oh you are too silly!" And Amy, greatly agitated, shook out Kathleen's bloomers and spread them on the chair back turned to a careless angle at the desk. She then smoothed out Kathleen's other clothes and laid them there too. Kathleen watched, surprise in her eyes, when the desk was bare.

She raised herself and Amy blushed deeper at Kathleen's breasts jumping about on the edge of the sheet.

Amy tucked the chair under the desk, lips pressed together in her bowed pink face.

"We'll go to see Aunty Daph. But you have to get dressed first."

Kathleen flopped back on the pillow and raised both arms above her head. "Oh, Amy, Amy! I'm so happy!" The words whispered their way through her full throat.

"With your new bed?" asked Amy.

"No. With Jim."

Daphne was no help in persuading Kathleen to stay at school.

Her face closed like a door on a room that gave little away even with the door partly open.

Amy said that Miss Parks, Kathleen's teacher, would like Kathleen to become a teacher too.

Amy watched Daphne's eyes fall to her lap and her mouth go in at the corners and the smudge of dark hair on her upper lip go darker.

It's Peter and because he was a teacher, Amy thought, wanting to put her arms around Daphne for comfort but afraid to bring on tears, or worse still, a rebuff.

"I don't know about teaching for a girl," Daphne said, jerking her body on her chair in a way Amy recognized as ridding herself, however temporarily, of her grief. I'm forgetting Peter, Amy thought. She never will.

Another jerk took her to the stove and the kettle, and encouraged, Amy tried again.

"This Miss Parks said Kathleen could be a teacher.

"If she leaves school she will start thinking about boys and get married too young."

Daphne prized open the lid of the biscuit tin and up rose a sweet smell of vanilla and butter. She still makes those biscuits Peter loved, Amy thought, pleased.

"I reckon she's thinkin' of them without leavin' school," Daphne said with a sideways cock of her head.

"She's in there lookin' at Helen's glory box."

At the end of the school year Kathleen came home with her case bulging with her used exercise books and a linen bag she had made for her library books bulging with more. She had her Intermediate Certificate in its envelope between two fingers.

Amy was already home from work and peeling potatoes, for Kathleen had spent the past couple of hours with Tina at her father's fruitshop, where Tina was now employed, partly as punishment for failing the examination, but mainly to save her father paying wages.

Amy heard the heavy thud of Kathleen's load as it hit her bedroom floor, and when she came to the kitchen she slipped the envelope behind the tea caddy, and brushed her hands one against the other, then flung herself down on a kitchen chair.

For a little while she appeared to hold a dream trapped to her face, looking past Amy's profile to the window over the sink. A potato jerked about in Amy's hand, refusing to be steady, the jerking knife close to cutting her. She did nick her palm for Kathleen jumped to her feet.

"Good on you, Amy!" she cried. "What's for tea?"

Kathleen went to work with Amy at Anthony Horderns in the book department. She squealed with joy when Amy told her her applications had been successful and she could start the following Monday.

She was passionately devoted to her job, smart and pretty in her navy blue dress buttoned from neck to hem and with a detachable white organdie collar. She washed her collars every second night and ironed them, with Amy admonishing her for adding to the electricity bill. But Kathleen paid ten shillings a week board, and Amy, who undertook the job of packing away Kathleen's school uniforms and books so that she was never given a glimpse of them, told her conscience life was much easier now.

Kathleen disposed of Jim a few months after she started work.

While they were both at school they were hardly able to afford any outings, even something as simple and cheap as a ferry ride to Manly. Once Amy asked Jim to tea at Petersham on a Sunday night, and one Saturday afternoon Kathleen and Jim were taken for a drive to Penrith with John and Helen in John's truck, a tight squeeze which added to their fun. John had to pay for their milk shakes after they watched a soccer game in a park. Kathleen longed for the time when she and Jim had pay packets of their own.

Kathleen was the first to get one, two weeks before Jim started as a clerk with the railways. Bursting with generosity she slipped four shillings into his hand before they set out for the Parramatta Roxy. Jim as a railway employee travelled free and Kathleen rushed forward to buy her own ticket, wanting to make the treat complete for him.

"We'll do this again soon. My shout," Jim said on their way home along Crystal Street, so tightly wrapped in each other's arms they fell over each other's feet, laughing so much that people stared, thinking they were drunk.

But when it was Jim's turn to pay he walked with his hands in his overcoat pockets and his hat tipped forward to nearly cover his eyes, and if Kathleen hadn't put an arm inside his she would have been left several paces behind.

Turning back her bed and shivering, partly with cold but mostly with disappointment, Kathleen channelled her anger towards Jim's mother. He gave her his pay packet unopened and she gave him back what she called his pocket money. He had brought her into Anthony Horderns to introduce her to Kathleen there. She was pale complexioned, wearing a close-fitting black felt hat that seemed to shrink her face. Kathleen, who like Amy thought about faces, was reminded of a cup with features drawn on it. The eyes were dark like Jim's, and darting from Kathleen's display of children's books to her organdie collar and back to the bare counter, their expression did not change.

"Do you read a lot, Miss Fowler?" she asked, frowning and shrinking her face even more. Kathleen was sure it would be considered sinful to admit she did.

The eyes that told nothing swept the floor to take in all the departments on show. Kathleen was pretty sure she was looking for Amy.

"Or do you sew like your mother?" Jim reddened and turned his body, pressed to the counter, from his waist, ashamed of having informed his mother of the domestic habits of the Fowler household. Kathleen liked him for this, but when she tried to thank him with her eyes he turned away further. In her disappointment, she was then unable to answer his mother, added to which was her confusion at hearing Amy referred to as her mother, since she still thought of her as a sister after years without her, and Amy's years at Lincolns feigning the sibling relationship.

Jim walked behind his mother on the way out, sheltered deep in his overcoat. But he turned his face as they were about to disappear and mouthed goodbye. Kathleen, happier now and serving a customer with a thirteen-year-old daughter with a copy of *Little Women*, began to look forward to their next night out at the pictures. It will be lovely like it was before, Kathleen thought, her fingers smoothing the brown paper lovingly around the book, shutting away the title and understanding the sorrow in the girl's eyes, as if there was a danger of losing it forever. But the mother allowed her to carry it off hugging it to her little hard chest, and old Mr Benson bowed between the book and Kathleen, who had used string sparingly, judging the right amount needed, and making a beautiful little loop with her fine long fingers. Some staff who had been there much longer than little Miss Fowler would have cut off enough to go twice around the parcel. Tch, tch.

In bed Kathleen tried to think of the good parts of the evening, but there were none. Jim had crouched in his seat at interval, and Kathleen's throat had ached for the potato crisps rustled by others around them. The only good thing she could remember at all about him was that goodbye he mouthed to her behind his mother's back on their way out of Anthony Horderns.

It had seemed a conspiracy, a secret message of love between the two of them. She sat up sharply in bed and saw it differently. He would love her only behind his mother's back, and soon most likely not even then. She turned her pillow over and cried into it for a little while, then scrubbed her face dry with the edge of the sheet and sat up again.

She mouthed goodbye to the wall opposite, then sliding deeply under the covers she slept soundly until morning.

For a long time afterwards Kathleen showed no interest in boys.

"Sometimes I wish I could change places with you Amy!" she said. "Go into materials!"

"Whyever?" Amy asked.

"So's I wouldn't have to serve M-E-N," she spelled the word. It seemed less distasteful that way.

Away from their counters they were seldom apart.

"Let's save on lights and I'll read in your bed!" Kathleen said once and fell asleep with the cover of the book pressed into her cheek. Amy stroked the mark away and curled up on her small portion of the bed, careful not to disturb her, and fell asleep crying a little with love.

Kathleen began to call Amy her Siamese twin. They packed their lunch together at the kitchen table and ate it together at midday; sometimes if the day was fine they walked up George Street to the park Amy used to cross to go to work at Lincolns when she lived with the Coxes. They looked at shop windows but never bought anything. Because of the discount for Anthony Horderns' staff they bought everything there. Ah-Ha, Kathleen called it because of the initials A.H.

"Ah-Ha!" she would greet Amy when they met to go home together, and "Ah-Ha!" she would say when she had an excuse to pass Amy's counter. No one within earshot took any notice.

"Never in a million years would they wake up to anything as simple as that!" Kathleen said of the staff.

"Without you Amy, life would be as dull as ditch water. Let's work all the weekend in the garden, shall we S.T.?"

Amy was surprised, since Kathleen liked to get away from the house at weekends, occasionally going straight to a movie matinee after work on Saturday, or with Amy to the Coxes on Sunday.

There was the chance then of an outing with John and Helen, although Daphne expected to have a turn now and again, and Mrs Cousins as well, and Helen's young brother was ready to set up a whine if he was left out.

Since the one seat accommodated four at a squeeze, there was usually an uncomfortable start, with John at the wheel and Helen beside him, and the others standing about trying to look as if they didn't care one way or another.

It was usually Daphne and Amy who stayed behind, glad if Mrs Cousins went. She was inclined to follow them into the Coxes' house, compensating herself for the missed ride by gloating over the coming nuptials, not attempting to hide her triumph that her Helen was getting a good hard-working man and Amy had none.

On the road John and Helen were triumphant too. Helen liked to travel with her hand between John's thighs, unacceptable behaviour if Mrs Cousins was looking on. John had to make a show of cheerfulness, as if he actually liked having Mrs Cousins there. But privately he was resolving to let her know once he and Helen were married that his mother-in-law would need to find another place for her great, fat arse.

Amy was doubtful that Kathleen would keep her promise to spend her free time working in the garden but she did, although there was an unusual start. She came out of her room, after shutting herself in there when they had finished their midday sandwich, wearing a new bathing costume. Amy was almost as surprised as when she'd found her in bed naked. The costume was fuschia coloured and Kathleen turned around at once to show her back naked to the waist. She put her hand to her back to finger the start of a shoulder strap. "One of Ah-Ha's best efforts, wouldn't you say, Amy?" She lowered her chin and eyes to look at her breasts running into the rich cloth. She pulled a piece with thumb and forefinger and it returned to its place with a little caressing slap. She touched the space between her breasts stroking at the fine stitching there, telling Amy to love them.

She put a foot on a kitchen chair, and her hands one on top of the other on a knee. Amy saw the dark shadow between her legs and sat herself abruptly on another chair. Her eyes willed the legs to close.

"I thought we were gardening," Amy said, gathering up their cups and banging the breadboard sharply on the table to free it of crumbs.

"We are!" Kathleen cried and ran to the back. Amy heard the clang of spade and hoe taken from the corner of the lavatory, and emerged to find Kathleen hoeing with great energy between the rows of young spinach. Amy checked the neighbouring fences for faces.

"You'll get it dirty! Please go and change!"

Kathleen stepped a pace backwards, stretching her body as if it were elastic, laughing as she hoed solidly. "Oh, I'm getting a suntan S.T.! Ready for the beach, you foolish old thing!"

Amy looked down at her own clothes, an apron such as May or Daphne would wear over an old mauve linen dress she often threatened to make into dusters.

"Go and put yours on!" Kathleen said, and flung the hoe from her and stretched full length on the grass under the clothesline, face downwards.

Amy's costume had no sleek finish like Kathleen's. It was in wool, bought while she was at Lincolns, not showing much back, with two little white buckles where the shoulder straps met the bodice she had thought quite wonderful at the time, and a skirt all the way round, not just in front like Kathleen's. It was in navy blue, a colour she suddenly hated.

If she put it on, her legs would seem even shorter with the skirt halfway down her thighs. Her knees were not good. She could not imagine the sun smiling on her skin as on Kathleen's, toasting it to the colour of pale honey.

Without looking, she saw her legs, shamefully shaded by her veins to a milky blue like separated milk.

She dug her fork into the earth and stood up, and heard the steps of the Misses Wheatley leaving the house. They saw Kathleen and stiffened. Kathleen raised a cool head and trailed cool eyes over them, showing them the back of her head when she returned it to the grass.

Amy was mesmerized by the Misses Wheatleys' legs. They were in grey lisle stockings, wrinkling about the ankles, especially on the thinner Miss Grace. In spite of the warm spring day they wore coats with fake fur collars, and their shoes were of black leather, Grace's with laces and Heather's with a tongue.

Amy raised the clothes prop as an excuse to look away from them. When the click of their heels could be heard no more, she went inside, sat on a kitchen chair and curled her legs under it, pulling her skirt over them. I won't go where there is a mirror, she told herself.

For if she looked in one she was sure the Misses Wheatley would look back.

Amy got a new costume, a dark green one with a zigzag pattern in white.

"You're dazzling, S.T.," Kathleen cried when she put it on.

"Shut up and pass me the coconut oil!" Amy said, blushing.

They spent a Sunday tanning in the backyard, and went to Bondi the Sunday after. Kathleen jumped from the stone edge of the walk along the beach front and laughed at the way the sand squeaked when her feet hit it. Amy laughed too but took the steps, pleased at the sight of her costume hugging the tops of her legs. If there hadn't been so many people about she would have pulled at the cloth and let it snap back cosily again.

But Lance Yates was looking. He was there with Allan coming from the beach, a rolled-up towel under his arm and Allan with his flung over a shoulder. Amy had time to feel glad their towels were out of sight in the beach bag Kathleen carried, one Tina had helped her make. The four of them stopped, Allan pushing his feet deeper into the sand, Kathleen dropping her bag down low enough to rest on her old sandals, Amy noticing the suitable footwear of Lance and wishing for some of her own.

Allan in shyness put a hand up and smoothed the hair on one side of his head, and felt for any that might be standing up at the back. He did not appear to be looking that closely at Kathleen, nor she at him, but Amy sensed they had seen a great deal of each other in the time it took for her to shape her mouth into a smile of greeting.

"My goodness me!" Lance said, and the oil trembled in his eyes and at the corners of his mouth, and even his teeth seemed to have received a light coating. Handy for the beach, Amy thought. He doesn't need coconut oil like the rest of us.

"We're just coming out," Lance said, regretting that they were.

"You're going in?" Allan, not yet bold enough to meet her eyes, addressed Kathleen's right shoulder.

Lance looked at the crowded beach around them, searching, Amy could see, for a place for them. She wondered if, when he found it, he and Allan would go and she would never see them again. She had to curb an impulse to reach out and take hold of Lance's wrist, a nice strong one attached to a yellowish hand. The thought caused her to redden and look at the sea, the black swimmers' heads like flies caught in foaming milk, remembering the

179

farm suddenly, and to her surprise not hating it. In fact, quite suddenly and unaccountably, she loved everything, including a small boy in an ugly woollen costume drooping from his hips with the weight of sand and water, beginning to dig with a wooden spade near her feet and lifting up a scarlet face and running nose. He had freckled limbs and spiky hair and Amy should have found him unattractive and shooed him off, but she could quite easily have scooped him up and hugged him.

All the groups of people looked handsome and happy. Amy was happy. She looked in vain for an unhappy face. People were going into the water smiling and coming out smiling, and dropping wetly into their little place and rubbing at their wet hair, some using old towels with few places thick enough to be effective. They smiled even wider looking for the most absorbent parts of their towels and upwards at the sun, thankful for its blessed rays. There was music in Amy's ears but none was playing anywhere. The people's voices were a singsong of sound, waves of it rolling up like the surf itself. The crash on the sand was like an orchestra warming up. Amy half expected the voices to die away and let the thundering music of the sea take over, and suddenly, miraculously, as if Lance had commanded it, there was only his voice she heard.

"Let's find somewhere quieter."

Amy saw the faces of Allan and Kathleen become eager. What's mine saying, I wonder? She pointed it to the sand in case they saw too much. They walked dodging the groups, stepping onto the edges of towels, even over the heads of children, around prams swathed in mosquito netting, sometimes kicking sand on tender pink backs.

"Wow!" the owners said but laughed, and Amy thought never again, never during the rest of her life would she see anyone frown, an unhappy face.

They were into the open, away from the crowds before she realized it, and looking up at the rocks resisting the swirling sea and two or three fishermen hung between the cliff and the sky, she needed to look back to check that the distance was there, it seemed she'd hardly walked at all.

"But it's away from the flags, Dad," Allan said and Amy caught Kathleen's smile, tenderly acknowledging his concern that she might be deprived of her swim.

"Oh, yes," Lance said, taking his first real look at Amy's costume, and then giving his head a little perplexed scratch in a way she remembered at Lincolns when he was looking at a new design for a line of knit shirts.

"We can sit in the sun for a while." Amy's murmured words covered those inside her head. He and I will sit in the sun. You others will go and swim.

They did that. Allan and Kathleen ran across the sand and hopped over the little waves breaking on the shore until they were in line with the flags that told swimmers to bathe between them. Amy watched them wade in, Kathleen taking the chill off the first plunge by dabbing handfuls of water on her legs, Amy thinking she should not worry at Allan watching closely while Kathleen bathed her thighs.

But her face warmed, not entirely from the sun's heat, and she experienced an odd sense of relief when Kathleen dived and swam like a bobbing fuschia quite far out, and Allan following was there if she got into difficulties.

She spread Kathleen's towel out in readiness for her and sat on her own, both hands on the sand propping her up. She could see only the bottom half of Lance, a tan fading out the yellowish colour of his legs, some little tufts of hair on his toes she found quite vulnerable. He wore black trunks with the emblem of a diving female shape above one thigh. She saw those too. Neither of them was saying anything and Amy felt surprise that this did not seem to matter.

In a little while she felt something run over her fingers, something like the feel of a small, gentle harmless animal, a sand creature perhaps scuttling for shelter, stopping and stroking, deciding not to go on. Amy did not look for quite a while, holding the anticipation to her, the surge of the sea abated now, less turbulent than the surge inside her.

She turned her hand over and his palm slid across hers, and then she turned her body around and laid her face on her arm and his face was closer to hers than it had ever been, and she thought never again in all my life will I be lonely or unhappy or frightened. Or alone.

Never alone again.

Lance insisted on driving them home. He could make a slight detour for a look at Lincolns. Amy could see the changes since she had left. Allan, with his nose beginning to peel and more sunburn cracking his lips, hoping he did not look too awful for Kathleen, reminded Lance there was nothing much added since Amy was there, other than new signwriting on the window of the dry cleaning shop, and the front window of the factory cleaned of its white paint and now displaying the uniforms of fighting men and women that had been made in the Lincoln factory. There was still need for a camouflage so that workers could not be seen at their machines. Lance and Tom overcame this by hanging the Union Jack and Australian flag to cover the opening. Allan, now working at Lincolns, wanted the American flag there too and Lance and Tom, by this time tolerant of the Americans, conceding that they had helped save Australia from a Japanese invasion, allowed it to be laid on the floor. Allan laid his head to one side, very close to Kathleen's shoulder, pointing out the rippled effect, almost as if the flag were flying from a mast. Amy, noticing the Land Army uniform, remembered Miss Sheldon with a little prickle of jealousy. She treated herself to a small inward chuckle. I quite like being jealous, she told herself.

"Victor has the keys to upstairs," Lance said as an excuse not to go there.

Amy, with a rush of love for his thoughtfulness, decided he was thinking of her, afraid she might feel pain at the sight of her old desk with Miss Ross's things on it, and Miss Ross's second best umbrella on the peg behind her chair.

She stole a glance at Lance's profile, pensive before the window, and saw the corner of his mouth digging into his cheek, and was struck by the marvel of kissing that mouth. I could not go on living if I was never to kiss that mouth, Amy thought, and stared into Kathleen's eyes, saying this without sound, and Kathleen returned the stare, puzzled, and looked at Allan as if he were her only security in a situation suddenly frightening her.

Allan and Kathleen sat in the back seat going to Crystal Street and Amy beside Lance. Only Kathleen said: "Oooh, my sunburn is sticking to the back of the seat," and Allan, deepening his own with his blush, thought her wonderful to make him feel less embarrassed about it.

Lance said they would not go inside and Allan scrambled over to sit in the seat Amy vacated.

Amy wandered to the back of the house and looked for a long time at a yellow rose turning its petals back, and thought of making a yellow dress with a collar turning back, touching her bare tanned shoulder with a crisp little peak. Wearing it for the first time for Lance to see.

When she turned her head Kathleen was on the path watching her. She shook her little purse in the air.

"I'll get some cold meat for our tea with the money we saved on fares," Kathleen called, nearly shouting as if she suspected Amy was suddenly hard of hearing.

Amy gave a little vague smile as if she would never have thought of such a thing.

She was getting into bed, calling out goodnight to Kathleen and Kathleen calling goodnight back when she began to feel something was missing.

Kathleen hadn't called her S.T. since they encountered Lance and Allan on the beach.

She never did again.

It was hard, nearly impossible, for Amy and Lance to have time on their own.

"Let me try and get the telephone on for you," Lance said, when Amy, knowing his habit of going to Lincolns at weekends, slipped away and found a phone box and Lance's amazed and joyful voice answered at the other end.

But she protested that it would be a long wait, for the production and installation of telephones for domestic use was low on the list of essentials.

"Blame the silly old war!" Amy said, hardly thinking of Peter at all.

But she was relieved, aware that Kathleen would know the source of the telephone, and at this stage she was trying to keep the relationship from her.

You are stalling, Amy Fowler, she said to her shining eyes in the mirror of the little cane dressing-table.

An opportunity to meet Lance came when Kathleen woke with a heavy cold and Amy, hoping her face did not give her away, insisted she stay at home in bed while Amy explained her absence to Mr Benson. She was aware that it was the exciting prospect of seeing Lance that made her bow in imitation of Mr Benson receiving the news. Keeping her eyes shut and her head lowered for a long moment, she did not know what expression Kathleen wore from her sick pillow.

She caught the tram to give her time to telephone Lincolns from a box and Lance said he would meet her in the tearoom at Anthony Horderns. Amy was joyful at the prospect of being seen with a man by her fellow workers, but this was tempered by the thought that some of them might tell Kathleen. It was lovely to get out of cutting lunch, Amy thought, relishing the asparagus on toast Lance ordered for her.

"We'll drive to the park and sit there for ten minutes," Lance said.

Ten minutes is not long enough to tell him Kathleen is my daughter, Amy told herself, relieved. They sat squashed together, holding hands, Amy with her shoes off and her toes rubbing gently at the new grass. Her feet were nicely tanned like her legs and Amy, looking at them, wondered how she had ever thought they resembled the Misses Wheatleys'. Lance was smiling down on her feet too. They're probably the prettiest feet he has ever seen too, Amy thought without shame at her conceit. She rubbed a cheek against the tweed of his coat.

"I always loved the clothes you wore," she said. "I used to say to myself, 'what will he be wearing today?' and watch out for you until I found out."

"I thought you hated me," Lance said.

She pressed her head hard into him as if she would make an opening to pour her love in and he would be convinced this way.

"The city is dancing," she said although her eyes were actually closed. "What is it doing, a waltz or a twostep?"

"You can dance, can't you? You said you couldn't, but I know you can."

"Did you hate me that night?" she whispered.

"I loved you that night!"

"Only that night?'

"Not only that night."

She had to put her feet into her shoes and stand up. She could keep her back to him. He might think her foolish if he saw her tears.

Kathleen was to learn about the meeting.

"Son," Lance had said to Allan on their drive home from work on the Monday after Amy had first telephoned Lance at the factory, "I won't keep anything from you."

Allan took off his tie and laid it on the back seat with his suit coat. He dressed up for work although he often mixed dyes, pressed clothes in the dry cleaning shop and shared many of the menial tasks of the more lowly paid. Lance wanted to impress on everyone Allan's grooming as a future boss. The good cut of his trousers said so and his

188

sleeve links of silver in the shape of a curled snake with a semiprecious stone for an eye terrified the new girls when his arm hovered over them, as they tried desperately to stop the fabric they were machining from curling like a slice of dry bread. Had they known it, Allan had a secret admiration for their skills, the way they made tiny invisible stitches and slipped thread through a needle eye and knotted the end faster than it took to blink. He didn't want to stand out from them, he wasn't comfortable having to hold his body a long way away from the dye vat to avoid splashes on his clothes. He didn't like it when his tie dangled close to the rim, since he had no free hand to grab it.

Allan was glad to be free of his coat and tie, and added to his comfort by wrenching his shirt buttons open. Lance saw this as a manly gesture, but left his own coat on, feeling like a kind of understudy, as if following the act would detract from its significance.

Of course he's a man! Lance sped past a tram, wondering if Allan, like him, felt pity for people travelling this way and thinking then of Amy and feeling light and happy, because she walked and was different from the ordinary hordes, superior and beautiful, swinging along on her slim strong legs.

It was Amy he was talking about to Allan.

"I love her, son. Perhaps you've seen."

There was silence but no chilling of the air between Allan's blue silk shirt and Lance's grey pinstriped suit coat.

"Yes, Dad, I know."

189

Lance put a hand on Allan's knee and shook it. "God, a man's lucky to have you!"

Lance told Allan about the lunch with Amy and how it had come about.

"Is she sick?" Allan cried, leaning towards the wheel and nearly bouncing onto it when Lance had to pull up to let a woman with a pram cross in front of him.

"No! She's looking wonderful!" Lance said forgetting Kathleen, picturing Amy with her shoes off.

"Is it the old one sick or the young one?" Allan cried, beating an elbow into Lance's side.

Lance, unable to believe anyone could think of Amy as old, began as evenly as he could to explain about Amy telephoning because Kathleen was sick in bed—

"But how sick? How sick?" Allan cried, and Lance was afraid Allan might wrench the car door open and leap out.

"She couldn't go to work, so it meant Amy could meet me. We had asparagus on toast." He thought with remorse of Allan eating the roast beef sandwiches Eileen had made for them that morning and how he hid his in the back of his desk drawer.

Allan put the back of his hand to his mouth and chewed a finger. "I'll go and see her tonight," he said in the voice of a man. "You can drive me there."

Lance's first thought was one of joy that he would see Amy. Then he saw himself outside the house crouched over the wheel in the dark and Amy running out angry with him, seconds after Allan ran in with chocolates—

"I'll take her something like a box of chocolates." Allan pulled what money he had from his trouser pocket, tipping his rump sideways to get it all out, and stirred it with a finger to count it.

"We can say we have to go back to the factory."

"No, we can't!" Lance pictured Eileen serving the mashed potatoes—her way of scooping each serve into a mound and spooning the peas to completely surround it. It made Lance impatient, she made such a business of it the food grew cold.

Now he felt a film of sweat on his forehead and an urge to take his hand from the wheel and slap it across Allan's face. But he bowed closer to the wheel appearing to go faster. Allan stiffened his back against the seat as if urging the car backwards to Kathleen.

He loosened his body only when the car stopped with a whoosh inside the garage. It was one cut into the side of the rise on which the house was built. The roof formed a deck opening into the house, and Eileen left the door open if the weather was fine and would start dishing up the meal when the whoosh was heard.

Allan thought he might cry at the imagined sound of Eileen's fork whipping hard inside the potato pot. He saw nothing of his father's face because of the dark.

Only the feel of him listening for the light feet of Amy. He twitched about ready to say it didn't matter, he did not expect to be driven to Petersham to see Kathleen.

But Lance put a hand on his knee. "I'll take you there after tea," he said.

33

They went out sometimes as a foursome on Saturday afternoons, Lance and Allan dropping Eileen off at her parents' place, then, on the pretext of returning to Lincolns, collecting Amy and Kathleen at Petersham.

Once they went to a picnic spot by the Parramatta River where Kathleen took off her shoes and screeched at the chill of the water, and Lance bought double ice creams for them all.

They stopped at Lincolns before Lance and Allan took Amy and Kathleen home, and turned west again to pick up Eileen.

Allan took Kathleen to show her the new clothes racks in the dry cleaning shop and new overhead cupboards for storing the solvents and spare iron.

He had given the cupboards a coat of paint and when he closed the doors tenderly Kathleen put a cheek on his upper arm and rubbed it.

"You are wonderful," she whispered. He pulled the transparent covering from the clothes rack and put it over their heads and kissed her.

Upstairs at the same time Lance kissed Amy.

They were by the switchboard and in a little while he turned to it and picked up the telephone, still holding her with one arm. The feel of his arm has changed, Amy thought, slipping out of it. He half turned his back to tell Eileen he would collect her in an hour. Trembling, Amy went and sat in her old chair and opened a desk drawer, then shut it at the sight of unfamiliar things.

She watched Lance's hand go up and smooth his hair at the back. He needs a haircut, she thought, with the pain of a woman who wanted to tell him as a wife would, but knew she hadn't the right.

When he put the phone down he went and stood behind her chair and kneaded her shoulders. She rubbed the back of her head on his stomach and thought again, like a wife, he should control the flabbiness, and felt sad again that she could not help him.

All of a sudden her shoulders went cold. The coldness began to spread to other parts of her, until she almost shivered.

For Lance took his hands away and stuffed them in his pockets and took a couple of paces towards the middle of the room.

There were footsteps on the stairs, Allan and Kathleen hurrying up laughing and making a lot of noise with their feet as if their exuberance was released that way.

They came in swinging clasped hands. Amy tried but failed to get her lips to smile. She got up and tucked the chair neatly under the desk. She turned from their questioning faces on the pretext of looking at her face in the mirror that once hung on the side of a filing cabinet. But the cabinet had been moved and she felt rebuffed as if this had been done to her on purpose.

Allan and Kathleen let go their hands and led the way on quieter feet down the stairs.

"Something happen?" Kathleen asked in that kind of voice that does not care too much about an answer.

She was folding washing brought in from the clothesline and making a pile on the kitchen table. She wore shorts and a blouse that slid a little over one shoulder. Most of the time she adjusted it but now they were at home she let it fall and left the strings at the neck untied.

The hollow between her breasts was visible through the opening. Amy half expected her to fling off the blouse and her brassiere too and allow the breasts to bounce in exuberance as her feet did on the stairs at Lincolns.

When the towels and underwear and their Anthony Hordern uniforms were in a neat pile Kathleen flopped down on a chair and laid her face on a rough towel on top.

"Amy," she said with her eyes closed. "He kissed me under the cellophane. I felt like a bride."

Amy got up from her chair and swept the pile of things from under Kathleen and carried them into the next room where there was a copper and laundry tubs. Kathleen heard the clatter of the ironing board (which John had shaped from an old door of a demolished building) being laid across the tubs.

"Amy!" Kathleen called. She had her face on the table now, one cheek upwards, her eyes still closed. "Give me back a towel. I need to smell the sun and the wind!"

I know what you want to smell, Amy thought, and sent the iron hard across a tea-towel, burning out the sweet smell of fresh grass and pure air.

"You got the huff Amy? Didn't he kiss you?"

Amy flung the iron onto its little stand and rushed on Kathleen, who was on her feet in time and around the other side of the table. She laughed, believing it to be a game. But Amy's face said differently. Her blue eyes glittered like chipped glass under her sweaty hair, and her breath blew out from a pouted underlip as she charged with her scarlet face first to one corner then the other.

Kathleen's face went sober and she grabbed a chair back for protection, then tangled with the legs, and when it seemed Amy was bearing down on her, pushed the chair towards her and ran past it. She got the front door open in time to escape, with Amy only yards behind her. She flew out the gate, slamming it shut almost on Amy's stomach. One of the Misses Wheatley coughed from an upstairs window.

Oh pull your head in, Amy cried inside herself, running into the house.

Two hours later Kathleen came in and saw the table set and a plate of salad at her place. Amy, seated at the table, was wearing powder and lipstick. Her hair was freshly done and she was in a clean blouse and her old but still respectable navy skirt.

"Did you get anything at Tina's?" she asked pleasantly.

"Two rotten pears and a dirty look from oily Uncle Ol," Kathleen said, cutting into a tomato slice and laying a piece on her darted-out pink tongue. "Thank you for my tea, Amy."

"You're very welcome," Amy said.

34

That night Kathleen wrote to her grandmother.

Dear Grandma, I read your last letter at Aunty Daph's. It seems to me the best way out of the situation is to send Patricia to us. It would be very good for Amy (I call her Amy all the time now). Unfortunately she has fallen for this married fellow and no good will come out of it, only heartbreak for poor Amy. Patricia here to set up with a job, clothes etc. will take her mind off herself. I will inquire at A.H.'s to see if there is anything. I have a junior helping me in books now, so it is too late for Patricia there. But something would turn up. Who knows I might get her in at Lincolns. As a matter of fact the son Allan and I are going out quite seriously. He's a good line and if I may say so, a good catch as he will take over the business one day. Talk it over and write to Aunty Daph when you make up your mind. They are all well there, John and Helen getting married next year if they can find a flat. We are lucky with this house. If Allan and I married (don't fall down in a faint) we could have the rooms the terrible Misses Wheatley have. I am always at Amy to get rid of them. But I think Allan's father (who likes me a lot I know) would probably want something better for his only son. I haven't met the mother, who is a churchy type. Allan goes but only to please her. Hoping to hear from you soon. Love to Lebby. Her turn next.

Kathleen (Allan calls me Kay)

PS Isn't it great the war is over?

The pink tongue that curled so eagerly around Amy's salad licked the envelope down and Kathleen put the letter in her handbag. She stretched out on her bed and stared at the handbag hanging from the knob of her wardrobe door. The wardrobe was new, she had persuaded Amy to approve the purchase on time payment when she got a raise for training little Nancy Whelan. Amy was quite jealous of me when I got an assistant before her, Kathleen said to herself, transferring the wardrobe to the second bedroom of the house she and Allan would share, and seeing herself stacking her offseason clothes in it.

Oh, life is pretty jolly good, she told herself with a great leap from the bed. And I'm in a letter writing mood! The legs of her chair skidded when she sat at her desk again. She wrote:

Dear Allan, My own sweet boy, how are you? I have an overwhelming desire to see you. As a matter of fact I *must*. We *must* meet to talk something over of a very urgent nature. My whole future depends on it. If I said *our* future what would my dear sweet boy say to that? But first our meeting. Where and when? Stand by the phone say, Wednesday, giving you time to get this letter and I will telephone from the box near A.H.'s, just after twelve o'clock. Should anything happen and my lunch hour be changed to one, please return then and stand by.

All my love, K.

PS When we meet I want your father there too. This is of vital importance for it concerns him nearly as much as it does us. K.

199

The meeting did not come off as Kathleen planned it.

Dudley's heart failed and he died at work, hand-stitching the lapels of a herringbone tweed sports coat.

"Grab the needle!" shouted the office manager Oscar Banks. He saw but could not reach Dudley with the appropriate speed because of the glass wall separating the office from the factory. Dudley slid downwards in his chair, his face pale as bread dough, the needle pointing menacingly from between two fingers.

Sydney Rivers of Rivers Exclusive Men's Tailoring dropped his scissors with a great clang and rushed to lift Dudley into what he hoped was a more comfortable position. Dudley's head lolled sideways into the collar of his shirt which Daphne had starched sharp enough to cut him. Dudley had thrust out his feet in the last movement his body made. His smallish feet seemed the most defenceless thing about him, and with his trousers riding up there was a lot of black sock showing and a piece of innocent white leg. His shoes were black and highly polished, placed together so much like a schoolboy's, it was a surprise not to see a school case nearby.

Word of Dudley's death reached Amy and Kathleen at Anthony Horderns fairly soon. Oscar, with an air of melancholy importance, took the tram to Annandale and put Daphne in a taxi to the hospital in Camperdown where Dudley's body had gone an hour earlier.

Someone at Rivers remembered Dudley mentioning a niece working at Lincolns (Rivers stocked Lincoln made casual wear on the shirts and underwear counter). Only when Amy was safely out of his house had Dudley acknowledged the relationship.

Oscar's young lady assistant, caught up in the same aura of melodrama as Oscar (and quite enjoying it as a change from the monotony of office routine), assembled her features into a suitable expression of concern and telephoned Lincolns.

Lance was with Victor at the door of Victor's office, and when he heard Miss Isobel Mackie say "If you mean Miss Amy Fowler she isn't at Lincolns any more," he moved over to the switchboard and took the receiver from her hand.

Ignoring the round eyes riveted on him and deciding he cared nothing for any of them anyway, seeing only the blue of Amy's eyes he said, "Yes, yes, I see. We'll pass the message on." He then ran down the stairs to find Allan.

It was close to midday on the day Allan was to stand by the telephone for Kathleen's call. They scrambled into

201

Lance's Buick and reached Anthony Horderns ten minutes before twelve, Allan letting out his breath in a great puff of relief.

The four of them went to lunch in the tearoom. Kathleen cried with Allan's arm around her shoulders, and Lance held Amy's hand beside her plate of curry and rice, having insisted on their ordering something substantial enough to help bolster their grief.

Torn between tenderness and boyish embarrassment at the first sight of Kathleen's tears, Allan silently agreed with Lance that it would be ill-timed to raise the subject of Kathleen's letter unless she did. "It wouldn't be in good taste just now," Lance had said, not admitting to himself that whatever it was, he didn't want anything disrupting his relationship with Amy.

Lance was concerned not only with training Allan in the running of Lincolns but utilizing the time they were together (mainly travelling to and from work) for character building. Although he and Allan were close, Lance felt uncomfortable much of the time over his affair with Amy, and he was unable to find words to justify it. It's no use though, he would tell himself, taking off his coat at home to sit down to one of Eileen's roast dinners. I cannot give her up and don't intend to.

Allan was disappointed that Lance attached so little importance to Kathleen's letter. He took it from Allan's hand and frowned over it almost as if it were an order form filled out by someone on their first day in the factory. He handed it back without saying anything, Allan wincing and blushing at the way the line containing "my own sweet boy" leapt out, as if Lance had folded the letter that way on purpose.

Allan began to think he should keep a few things to himself concerning Kathleen. Perhaps Lance was jealous because she was younger and prettier than Amy. That was probably it, Allan thought, making no secret of the tender way he folded the letter and put it in his shirt pocket.

In Lance's own (secret) words he had "gone off" Kathleen. He suspected she was looking to Allan as a substantial meal ticket. He saw that Amy was afraid of her. When he proposed a meeting with Amy he watched her mind flick to Kathleen, mentally accommodating her. He thought often of a time when Kathleen would not be around. He did not know where she would go or what effect it would have on Allan, but he dreamed of Allan meeting another girl and the relationship dissolving amicably (so as not to upset Amy).

Lance saw Kathleen now with her wet eyelashes resting on her cheeks and her cheek very close to Allan's shoulders. I would dearly love to tell her her nose is red, he thought. He saw her lift her eyelids now and again to see what other of Anthony Horderns staff was observing her. She'll get a great kick out of the funeral, Lance thought. She's just the type.

Lance told Eileen he was going to the funeral. He lied about it. He said that Syd Rivers had asked for a good representation of people in the clothing trade to honour Dudley's memory, since Dudley had been a tailor for thirty years, most of the time with Rivers. Because Rivers was a good customer of Lincolns Lance said he should go. The funeral was at two o'clock on Saturday afternoon. Eileen could not see why Lance had to take Allan and sulked through their early lunch. Since the funeral was in Annandale and her parents' place only a few miles farther west she suggested she and Allan spend their time there while Lance was at the church and cemetery.

Allan stopped eating his meat pie (Eileen always bought pies with the Saturday shopping to save cooking lunch) and watched the gravy ooze onto his plate, terrified at the outcome of the proposal. But Lance squared his shoulders in a way he had when he was about to deliver a sound argument, and said that Allan had never been to a funeral, and since he would be faced with this kind of thing in his business life, he should learn the correct procedures now. It was Allan's turn to square his shoulders at this extension of his responsibilities. Eileen saw the manly gesture and in her pride relented. A good thing it was a Protestant funeral. If it had been a Catholic one she would have put her foot down, Eileen told herself.

Lance had further informed her that he would not be home until late in the evening, so it might not be worth her while cooking tea for them. Victor had been off Thursday and Friday with one of his bad chest colds, and Lance needed to spend a couple of hours on the accounts. It would be an opportunity to acquaint Allan with that side of Lincolns. In a fresh rush of pride Eileen failed to perceive the unlikelihood of Allan learning anything worthwhile leaning over Lance's shoulder with his thoughts somewhere else, in this case on Kathleen. Kathleen's existence had so far been kept from Eileen, something else Allan was beginning to resent, since he had a strong desire to show Kathleen off and to curb his mother's habit of pushing him towards girls at the church.

Of course neither Lance nor Allan went to Lincolns. They collected Amy and Kathleen from the Petersham house and went to St Stephen's Church of England, then to Rookwood Cemetery for the burial.

"Oh dear, this dreadful place!" moaned Kathleen in Allan's ear, as if the overgrown graves and broken headstones and upturned jam jars, long empty of their flowers and rimmed with greenish slime, were no fit resting place for the uncle she despised.

Afterwards they went to the Coxes for sandwiches, made in large quantities by Mrs Cousins, while Helen in green linen with large white buttons holding down four large patch pockets clung to John's arm throughout both ceremonies, dabbing at her eyes with a lace handkerchief on hire from her glory box.

Daphne's tightly held jaws relaxed a little when Lance laid a light hand at the back of her waist, holding a cup of tea in the other.

"You were a good wife. He had a good life with you, I'm sure of that." Lance was pleased Allan was within earshot to benefit from this example of etiquette suitable in cases of bereavement.

After a suitable pause, and at a signal from Kathleen, the toe of her shoe prodding his ankle, Allan asked Lance if it would be alright to go across to the park for a while. Kathleen put on a wan expression as if her grief was impossible to bear in the crowded room.

Daphne put a handkerchief to a wildly working mouth.

"He went there every Saturday to watch the cricket. Never missed."

"He never said much. But he thought a lot," Mrs Cousins said.

The quaver at the end of the sentence was swallowed in the clink of china, as Mrs Cousins, mixing sentiment with the practical, swept a half row of sandwiches from one plate to fill another.

Lance told Daphne he would take Amy to Petersham, then "slip" across to Newtown to attend to something at Lincolns. Would she tell Allan when he returned that he would call for him on the way back to Randwick? Daphne, watching Amy's back and her raised arms as she put on her little navy straw hat with the binding of pale gold on the brim, did not notice that Lance made no reference to Kathleen, who, he suddenly decided, could find her way to Petersham by any method she chose.

In her bedroom, Amy began to unbutton her yellow dress which reached high to her throat and had a little stand-up collar piped in yellow and white stripes. Lance took her hands away and finished the job, and she noticed how deft his fingers were, hardly fumbling at all.

She put her head right over his shoulder for she was nearly as tall as he, and her lips were pressed into his warm back, which was rippling gently with the unbuttoning.

"I'm tired of waiting," was all she said.

Going home in the car, Lance and Allan each thought about telling the other what had taken place when Lance took Amy to Petersham and Allan took Kathleen to the park.

They had travelled to within a mile of Randwick when Allan, feeling he might burst from his navy blue suit, suddenly yelled out: "Dad! Pull over!"

Lance ran the car under a straggling gum beside a park where several small boys with shirts hanging out waded home through long grass, arms around homemade cricket bats and stumps, and a woman pushed a bumbling pram with a child inside, clinging with fat dimpled hands to the sides.

Lance took the scene in briefly, looking at the woman for a resemblance to Amy, disappointed he couldn't see the child's face without understanding why, then turned his attention to Allan.

Allan's face was quite red, and he plucked at the cloth of his trousers over his knees. Lance ran his hand around the rim of the steering wheel and slapped it lightly. His little smile contained a recollection of Amy's tousled head coming out from under her peeled-off yellow dress, and how hurriedly she had smoothed her hair, more embarrassed about that than her near nakedness.

"They're not sisters at all, Dad!" Allan said with great urgency.

"I know," Lance said.

"She told you!" Allan cried as if Amy had betrayed Kathleen.

"She didn't have to," Lance said. He started up the car and Allan called, "Wait!"

But Lance said, "Son, I know a lot more about women than you," and turned the nose of the Buick towards Randwick.

John drove Kathleen to Petersham, silent most of the way, not sorrowing so much for Dudley as fearing Helen's mood on his return home. She had flounced to the kitchen when Mrs Cousins ordered her to help clean up after the meal, and John felt his manhood might be in question since he had not insisted on bringing her for the ride. At Petersham, Kathleen slammed the truck door hard, and once inside the house threw her sailor hat on Amy's lounge.

Amy was in one of the chairs in her petticoat with bare feet and legs, thinking of the chair back as Lance's chest and how she rolled her head around on it, and stretched her legs against his yellowish ones when their lovemaking

208

was done and they both knew they must dress and he must go. But for Kathleen, he could be here still, she thought, and lowered her eyes, afraid her resentment might show.

After a moment she opened them on Kathleen's flushed face, with eyebrows at odd angles like tarantula's legs above eyes cold with blue chips.

Lance had ignored her when he called for Allan. "We must go!" he called to Allan who scrambled into the car and (Kathleen thought) gave an almost resentful look in her direction as if she were at fault. He was all tenderness and sympathy in the park, blaming Amy if anyone for the deceit; he seemed proud of her for her confession. He couldn't change an opinion as quickly as that, Kathleen thought, fearful that he had.

Then John hadn't wanted to bring her home to Petersham; the dual rejection made her want to lash out at Amy, soft and pretty there in her chair like a newly fed gold and white kitten.

"Greasy Guts is not strong on manners, Amy, be warned of that!"

She shed her shoes by dragging them by the heels along the carpet.

Amy did not say anything. Her lips and eyes stayed tender.

"Amy!" Kathleen called, banging a heel on the floor. Amy slid downwards in her chair and spread her knees under her petticoat and thought, he might have got me with child. You never know, but I don't need to think about that just now, only about the next time. Please God, oh please, let it not be too far off.

"Amy!" Kathleen shouted, very straight of back and leaning very far forward. "They know about us!"

"You told him," Amy said quite pleasantly, as if she was merely making polite conversation.

"The deceit was terrible!" Kathleen shouted, as if Amy needed to be stirred to angry argument.

"Then there is no more deceit," Amy said, shaking out her hair and pressing both hands to the back of her head. The gesture said a big debt had been paid, a long illness had been cured. Freedom was beautiful.

"Did you tell him?" Kathleen asked, her eyes on Amy's quiet face and lowered eyelids.

"I didn't need to." Amy opened her eyes very wide and looked straight into Kathleen's. "He saw the stretch marks on my belly."

"How disgusting! What did he say?"

"Nothing. He just kissed them."

It was nearly six months before Amy became pregnant.

Every month when she discovered she wasn't, she felt let down, as if she was cheating in her love for Lance, then in a little while she would feel relief that she did not have to face the trauma of a pregnancy. I guess I must be a little mad, she decided.

Patricia came in the winter, fifteen and smart in a navy blue coat with silver buttons.

"Dad bought it for me," she said, running a finger along the stitching on one of the side pockets. Amy waited for her to raise her eyes to see if this was some sort of joke. She did look up, then quickly away to a pair of fat china cats on the mantlepiece that Lance had bought for Amy when they passed through the china and glass-ware department one day on their way out of Anthony Horderns. Patricia's face, a nice open one with some

211

freckles and a brown fringe, went soft at the sight of them, then wistful, wishing for a pair like that for her grandmother.

"He's the yardman at the Moruya hotel," Patricia said, taking in the rest of the lounge room with travelling brown eyes.

Amy sat. Kathleen did too, and her face said, this is indeed interesting.

"What's he look like?" Amy asked, then asked herself why did I say that when it doesn't matter at all.

"Alright," Patricia said. "Fat." Then she looked down on her coat as if repenting and stroked a button. "Not real fat. Just a bit."

"Is he by himself?" Kathleen asked. Amy flinched. Patricia looked puzzled.

"He was," she said. "He was sweeping the yard."

In a moment she broke the silence. "Norman told us he was there so we went to see him."

"Who went?" asked Amy.

"Granma and I." She went and stroked one of the cats. "Then he came out to the farm to see Lebby and brought me the coat." For the first time she looked in Amy's face. "Because I was coming here."

Norman had brought Patricia to Sydney, and arriving late in the evening took her to Daphne's, then caught a tram back to Central to get a train to Queensland. Norman was having a holiday with Fred who was now working on a sugarcane farm outside Gympie. Fred had not gone home to Diggers Creek after the war. He met an Army nurse while in camp at Enoggera and the girl's father gave him work after he was demobbed.

Fred sent twenty pounds to Norman to come north for the holiday, the first in his life. It was partly an expression of gratitude that Fred had avoided active service and Norman had stayed at Diggers Creek with the old pair, dreary as the prospects were compared to his life with Beryl. But Fred asked Norman not to "let on" to Beryl where the holiday money came from.

"Beryl wants us to get a place of our own and she wants to keep on nursing after we're married," Fred wrote. "It's only fair for me to watch the pennies too. Mum's the word, as we used to say."

Gus described his future daughter-in-law as a bloody tightwad and wanted nothing to do with any woman who went out to work after she was married.

John and Daphne brought Patricia to Petersham, where they were received by an astonished Amy and a surprised but subdued Kathleen, doing her best to monitor the conversation to ensure there was no reference to the letter she had sent to Diggers Creek, suggesting Patricia come to Sydney.

In a little while Amy, feeling like a swimmer trying to keep afloat with an eye on the shore at the same time, sat abruptly on the arm of one of her chairs. Controlling the restlessness of her hands by pinning them between her knees, she murmured that it was perhaps unfortunate she was going out that evening, it being Saturday and the rare event of a date at the movies with Lance.

"No need for anyone to get up to boiling point," Daphne said, patting the space on the lounge beside her and sending an invitation with her eyes to Patricia to sit there.

She brushed Patricia's overlong fringe out of her eyes.

"She's the livin' spit of May at the same age," she said. "We'll get a pair of scissors to that fringe. Where has John got to?"

Amy was glad to go and look for John. She reached the kitchen as his big boots crunched the gravel outside the kitchen door.

He had been inspecting the back garden, a little wistful of face, Amy thought, since he no longer came at weekends to work with her. He looked around the kitchen wistfully, still seeing the small jobs he'd done for her, the last a board with hooks where she hung her two saucepans and frying pan. He noticed a loose knob on a dresser door, waggled it and said he would get some wood glue from the truck and fix it.

Amy watched while he took the knob off, then set it in place with the glue applied, lining it up with its companion with a measuring eye. She wondered if he was thinking of Helen, doing jobs of this kind for Helen.

When he drew in his lips to whistle through them she decided he wasn't, that he had no thoughts at all beyond making the knob secure and leaving no smudge of glue on the scrubbed pine. His marriage to Helen was, Amy believed, Helen's idea. One day perhaps he would look down on the heads of his children and ask himself why did I do that? And then he would look at Helen, a stranger there, plump and comfortable in an old dress, or thin and nagging in an old dress.

What way will it be then for Lance and me? she asked herself, but seeing no answer anywhere and wanting to change the subject in her mind went into the lounge room.

She saw with surprise Patricia's brown head in the curve of Daphne's arm. It's terrible the way I keep forgetting my children, Amy thought, sitting gingerly on the small space left on the lounge, wanting to take hold of Patricia's hand but feeling she had no right to.

Patricia went to live with Daphne.

A week later Amy was pretty sure she was pregnant.

Daphne knew even before Lance.

Amy got up very early one Sunday morning, about three weeks after Patricia came, to walk to the Coxes. She left a note for Kathleen who was still asleep, saying they were out of milk and she would look for a shop open at that hour and buy a bottle.

She had slept hardly at all. She alternated between joy at the thought of the coming child and terror at the difficulties she would face. She tried to remember when her stomach began to swell with the other children and had to face the fact that with each successive pregnancy her waist thickened earlier.

She sat up quite wildly in bed and clutched her middle as if to try and curb the rising that had already begun. She looked through the window, her wan face on the wan night. Her pillow had grown icy cold without her head, and back on it she rubbed it with her cheek, making it colder with her tears.

Why wasn't Lance here beside her to share her secret? Oh, the baby will be beautiful! A boy, a boy, a son! Oh, I'm so glad, so glad! Lance! Lance! Be glad too! Whatever will become of us! She pulled the blankets over her head and cried herself to sleep.

No one was up at Coxes when she got there. The back door was never locked so she went in that way.

"Who?" Daphne called the moment Amy's feet touched the step into the hall.

"Me, Aunty Daph," Amy said and took off her coat at the bedroom door.

"I came out for milk." She looked down at her shoes and saw with half her worrying mind that they would need repairing soon.

Daphne's hair was loosely plaited over one shoulder. It should have made her look younger, but instead she looked older in her pintucked white nightgown than in her house dress with the hair scraped back in a bun. Dudley's pillow was on the bed when it was made up in the daytime. At night it rested on a chair. Amy saw it tossed away like Dudley's lifeless body and tears came into her eyes. She moved it gently and sat on the space left.

Daphne raised herself in bed watching. There seemed nothing for Amy to do but turn her hands palms upwards in the lap of her tweed skirt and stare at the button fastening it to one side, wondering if she only imagined the button-hole stretched with strain. A car rumbled past and Amy wondered who would have what mission so early in the

217

morning, and then thought it might be someone going to hospital to have a baby. A silence followed, then the rattle of a milkman's cart, and Amy switched her thoughts to the need to get milk. She considered running out and hailing the driver, except that Daphne's expression riveted her to the chair.

"How long you gone over?" Daphne asked.

Amy jumped only slightly; it was hardly noticeable. Her hands gripped and then released the chair arms. She got up, leaving her shoes to fall over, and got into the bed in Dudley's old place and howled like a terrified child.

Daphne took her in her arms. Amy smelt moth balls and flesh, some mustiness and hair with a faint odour of soap, and felt a hard bone in Daphne's shoulder against her chin and the soft sponge of Daphne's cheek on her forehead.

Daphne's hand pressed Amy's head onto the end of her pillow and the other hand pinned her body to the bed.

"Cry quiet," she whispered. "So's not to wake the others."

"Is Patricia alright?" Amy asked, wiping her eyes dry by rubbing them in Daphne's hair.

"Course she is," Daphne said. "She starts a job Monday."

Amy hit Daphne's nose with her sharply raised head. "I won't be able to work soon. Whatever will I do?"

Daphne swung herself out of bed with the speed and energy of an eighteen-year-old. She had belted her flannel dressing gown at the waist in the time it took Amy to sit up, surprise chasing some of the tragedy from her face.

"I'll come back with a cuppa tea," Daphne said. But Amy scrubbed her face dry with a piece of sheet and followed Daphne to the kitchen.

"I should be thanking you for helping Patricia get a job," Amy said, unable to suppress the self-pity in her voice. "I can't seem to think of anything but—you know. It." On the couch now she rubbed one stockinged foot upon the other.

Daphne gave the handle of the kettle a little shake as if this would hurry the boiling. "There's a few worries storin' up here too, make no mistake about that." She unhooked two cups and set them on saucers with hardly any noise in spite of the angry jerking of her arms.

Worries! Amy heard the word with an odd sense of relief. There were others with worries then, apart from her. She watched for Daphne's grey flannel shoulders to turn so that she could see her face.

She saw the changes since Dudley's death. Daphne's complexion had always been muddy, now the muddiness had darkened. There was more grey in her hair, still hanging loose.

"You should put a bit of colour on that gown," Amy said, making her eyes very round in a bid to restrain her tears.

Daphne looked down at herself.

"Just a bit of contrast on the collar and cuffs," Amy said. "There'd be something in your work basket if we looked."

Amy went for Daphne's wicker sewing basket, which was leaning to one side with age, its lid like a hat covering eyes ashamed that it could no longer maintain a youthful pose. Amy searched among the ends of material, until she caught up a roll of braid and allowed it to unfold, her face taking on a pleased look that the piece was long enough, and the red and black pattern on white ideal for a trimming. Daphne peeled off her gown and Amy caught it as Daphne tossed it towards the machine and set to work, sniffing just a little, and with the tip of her tongue in the corner of her mouth to catch a tear if one or two fell. "Two strips on the collar, one on the cuffs and across the pocket. I'll only need to unpick the pocket part way down." Amy found Daphne's scissors in a machine drawer and clattered them on the raised flap, and wriggling her bottom on her chair, set her feet firmly on the treadle.

Daphne, looking terribly large in her nightgown, put a cup of tea at Amy's elbow and carried her own to her bedroom. The machine was running and Amy's head was bowed close to the braid when Daphne returned with her hair unplaited over her cardigan. The whirring machine and the slosh of water in the bathroom and the clatter of brush and comb on the marble shelf under the mirror made Amy wonder for a moment if anything was really different about the morning.

Patricia heard too and came out with the quilt from her bed wrapped around her.

"Your Ma'll have to make you a dressing gown," Daphne said, the braid now in place on the pocket reflecting the brightness in her guarded eyes.

Patricia swept the quilt around her in sudden joy.

"Mind you keep that off the floor," Daphne said sharply, and Patricia went to the couch and lay there arranging the quilt fussily over herself, as if she were both nurse and patient. Daphne took oatmeal from the food safe and began to mix it for porridge. Amy, now securing the pockets on the gown, felt her stomach hollow suddenly and her mouth fill with saliva. I will get sick of a morning soon, the same as with the others, Amy thought, in sudden panic that she was already sick. If I'm still sick at work whatever will happen? She looked at the solid figure of Daphne to allay her fears.

Patricia snuggled under the quilt. "I'll get material for a dressing gown with my first pay," she said.

Daphne gave a little snort of laughter. "What next is coming out of that pay, I wonder! You've already bought Farmers and Anthony Horderns out!"

I don't know what job she has, or where it is. What a mother I turned out to be, Amy thought. She laid down the scissors and put her hands to her face, pushing the flesh up to make two glittering blue slits of her eyes.

"If you feel like layin' down, go off and I'll finish that," Daphne said.

Patricia shot up from the couch and fixed her gaze on Amy, who with a display of control began to hand stitch the end of the braid into place. Patricia lay down again.

"Off you go miss, make your bed and when you are done give that John a yell. He'd lay there forever if you let him. Things'll be different when he's married to that one." She sat with her knees wide. "I'll say they'll be different."

"You'll miss him when he's out of the house," Amy said, looking down on her needle, knowing there were added words on Daphne's face, a little afraid of reading them.

221

Daphne got up and flung a cloth on the table and took spoons from the dresser drawer and set them with little thuds in four places.

"Nothing for me, Aunty Daph," Amy said. "I'll get back."

"John might take you," Daphne said. "Asking Madam first, of course."

"No, I'll walk and get the milk on the way."

"Well, walkin's good for you." Daphne gave the porridge its last hard, rapid stir.

Amy walked rapidly too towards home. It's true then, she thought, really true. I have to start to believe it.

When Amy reached the Petersham house Kathleen was sprawled by the kitchen table, her chin close to Amy's note as if it were written in a foreign language and required deep concentration to interpret it.

Amy dumped the bottle of milk beside it. "I went to Coxes and put some trimming on Daphne's grey dressing gown, and half promised to make one for Patricia and got all their news."

Kathleen pulled a face like a child anticipating a dose of disagreeable medicine.

"Patricia has a job but I came away without finding out what it was." Amy sat pulling her arms out of her coat and shrugging it off to rest it on the chair back. She spread her legs out and Kathleen looked on with distaste.

"You're getting very slovenly Amy," she said, sitting erect and crossing her knees and draping an arm over her chair back, letting a hand trail elegantly from her wrist. She inspected her nails one by one.

"You haven't heard the rest of my news," Amy said, and Kathleen swung her hand back and forth as if to wave away whatever was coming.

Amy went to the dresser for a packet of cereal and shook out a plateful and reached for the milk. "I need this food," she said, looking at Kathleen with round eyes and full round cheeks. "I'm having a baby."

"Oh, you're not!" Kathleen said and looked at her nails again. "Don't put the cornflakes away. I'll get some in a minute." She disposed of her elegant pose and raised a knee to sit her chin on it.

"God, life's a bore, isn't it?"

"Quite the opposite I think," Amy said, dumping her plate in the washing-up dish. "Will you have tea and toast if I make it?"

"If you want it. Or crave for it. Certainly."

"No craving. Just necessary nourishment."

"God Amy, you're a fool," Kathleen said.

Amy kept her back turned, filling the kettle, lighting the gas, getting out the toaster Lance had bought them from a factory beginning to manufacture peacetime goods again. She was quite a while turning round. When she did tears were pouring down her face.

Kathleen got to her feet, astonished. "You are then? You're not!"

Amy pulled out a chair with her foot to sit and hold her face. Tears ran through her fingers. "Oh, I can't stop crying!" She reached for an apron hanging from a hook to mop her face.

"I cried with all of you!" Amy sobbed. "For days and days."

"That's something to look forward to," Kathleen said, sitting again, sprawling her legs, turning her toes in. "My God, Amy, you're selfish!"

Amy swallowed and held her throat and opened her eyes very wide, the whites showing up the reddening rims.

"You heard me! Selfish!" Kathleen stood, then sat with the legs of the chair tearing the floor. "Do you realize what this will do to Allan and me?"

Amy's face said she had given no thought to this.

"You are the most totally selfish person I know!" Kathleen shouted, on her feet again the better to raise her hands to tick off the fingers of one with the forefinger of the other. "There's his wife, there's him, for what he's worth, there's Allan, there's me, just for a start!

"There's Patricia dumped on Aunty Daph!" Kathleen looked back for her chair to avoid missing the seat and this time sat erect with her feet together like a schoolteacher dealing with an errant pupil.

"Which reminds me, since you dumped us all, who will you dump this one on?"

Amy gave her head a little tired shake as if she had not yet reached this point in her planning.

"You're probably not pregnant at all, you know! You want to be to break up his home and break up Allan and me, you're imagining it! Amy you're a harlot! A scheming harlot!"

The kettle whistled and they both allowed it to go on, looking at it as if they expected it to shriek itself out if they waited long enough. In the end Kathleen snatched up the teapot, and clicking the little metal lid open, poured in the stream of smoking water.

"After I've had this I'm going to Tina's and we'll walk to Hyde Park. The spruikers there, mad as they are, make more sense than any conversation here with you!"

"I thought you'd be going somewhere with Allan," Amy said.

"Oh, just listen to her! 'Going somewhere with Allan.' My shame is so great I'll never face him again!"

She went swiftly to her room, banging the door behind her, and went close to the mirror door, her chin nearly touching the glass while she searched for flaws in her complexion, and with her fingers plucked at stray hairs disturbing the line of her eyebrows.

"I'm sick of the creep anyway," she said to her reflection.

It was nearly three months before Lance was told.

Amy was not sick, her figure was slow to change. She decided to enjoy the few outings they had together.

Kathleen was not seeing Allan. She wrote and told him it was better that they part.

"Under circumstances beyond my control," she wrote with relish and repeated to herself many times, even after the letter was posted.

Allan rushed with it to Lance, alone at the time in Victor's office.

"She doesn't mean it! She can't!" Allan cried. His words seemed to come from his eyes. They were larger than his mouth and growing wider with the plea in them for Lance not to believe it either. Lance took the letter and going to the partition he rapped on the glass, to bring about the instant lowering of girls' heads and the rattling of machines like a burst of gunfire.

That afternoon Lance took Allan to a jeweller he knew personally in King Street, and although the sign said "Quota Sold for Today", Lance bought Allan a wristwatch.

On the way home to Randwick in the car, Lance noticed that Allan allowed his suit cuff to ride back so that the watch was not lost to sight. It seemed the face winked at Lance every time he glanced down at Allan's hand lying on his knee. He needed to curb an urge to wink back.

Nearing home Allan broke a long silence. "I'll have to go and see her, Dad," and Lance caught another wink as Allan gripped his kneecap.

Lance was very calm at the wheel. "Bide your time, son," he said as he changed gears.

But his calmness had the effect of churning panic inside Allan's chest. Watch or no watch, he thought, suddenly allowing his cuff to cover it, I'll go and see her at lunch time tomorrow.

Joe Miller was new at Horderns and worked on window displays. He had very black hair and a white skin which did not make him look effeminate as you might expect. He was a little overweight but tall enough to carry the extra flesh, and he had reddish lips like a girl's. He smiled a lot, showing his white, even teeth. He wore white shirts and a dark suit and Kathleen, describing him to Patricia, said he looked like a cross between a magpie and a penguin.

"But he's absolutely gorgeous!" Kathleen said. "When he's in the window people stop and stare thinking he's the model. Truly!"

Patricia got a job in a corner grocer's store in Annandale where Daphne had dealt since she and Dudley moved into Wattle Street before John was born. Clyde and Maude Campbell were about to put a card in the window bearing the words "Junior Wanted" when Daphne came in with Patricia for the dozen wooden clothes pegs she'd been promised when the first postwar supply was delivered.

Maude said: "I reckon we could give her a go," then yelled: "Clyde," in such a loud voice Patricia jumped and went very red and held onto the edge of the counter, in sudden terror that her behaviour might put an end to her chance of employment

Clyde came out in the white calico apron Daphne had never seen him without in twenty years, the only change in his long, sad face a curiosity bringing a small spark to his dull brown eyes when he rested them briefly on Patricia.

"This here is Daphne's niece," Maude said, measuring sugar into a dozen brown paper bags set upright on the counter. There was no need to stop work she considered, her round red arms wobbling flesh as she shovelled sugar into the bags then slapped them on the scales.

"If she's honest and a good worker like the rest of the family she'll do. Anyway we'll give her a go." She did not look at Clyde for confirmation or denial and Patricia did not dare to. There was no change in his expression anyway as he pulled the filled bags to the opposite end of the counter and folded the tops down, applying a dab of glue with a little brush, not allowing so much as a grain of sugar to escape. Watching, Patricia forgot her nervousness. She thought if she were doing a job like that she would ask for nothing more in the world.

Kathleen came straight from work the next Saturday and Patricia closed her bedroom door on the two of them. In their exuberance, Kathleen with Joe Miller and Patricia with her job, they leapt one on either end of the bed, the springs shrieking loudly enough to cause Daphne to call from the kitchen: "Steady there! There's no money box I can empty for a new bed, thank you very much!"

"The mood's been black all the week!" Patricia whispered, rolling her eyes towards the ceiling, but rolling Daphne out of the way too to get to the more important topic of Joe Miller replacing Allan Yates in Kathleen's affections.

Kathleen flung a hand across her face, which was tipped over the side of the bed, as if Allan Yates were a troublesome fly to be brushed off before it had a chance to settle.

As he'd intended, Allan reached Anthony Horderns in time for lunch, and just in time to see Kathleen come out of the big wood and glass doors leading to the street hand in hand with Joe Miller.

His first impulse when he saw Kathleen and Joe Miller together was to plunge through the pedestrians on the footpath and rush between them. But he stopped and allowed himself to be bumped and jostled, miraculously keeping his balance with heels and chin raised until the two dark heads bobbed out of sight. Then he turned to break into a half run, jostling and bumping in his turn, sometimes breaking through the joined hands of a mother and young child, the mother indignantly calling after him and others picking up her protesting cry.

"Watch it Buster!" cried an old man, shaky on his legs, when Allan plunged into a thick knot of people pressing towards a stationary tram. Allan saw the tram was marked Railway and stood at the back of the crowd panting and close to tears, looking away as the heads turned to stare at him. In his seat he forgot Kathleen for a moment, in his enormous relief at finding he had enough money in his pocket for the fare.

He caught another tram at Railway Square bound for the eastern suburbs. He was crying when he went into the kitchen and found his mother shelling peas and reading the old newspaper they were wrapped in.

"Did you lose your watch?" she cried, getting to her feet with some difficulty, for she was growing stouter and her stomach was fairly well wedged under the table.

Allan, shaking his head, was blubbering freely now, as he had done as a small boy reaching the shelter of the house after losing a fight in the neighbouring backyard. He went straight to his room.

On her way to the telephone Eileen heard the rattle of bed springs and a great sobbing sniffle, as much of relief as sorrow.

Lance was very calm at the other end of the telephone.

"Leave him be," he said. "It's his first bout of puppy love. He'll meet another girl."

231

Eileen trotted towards the kitchen in a glow of love. She had foolishly expected Lance to order Allan back to work at once. She pictured him at the telephone (she knew he was in the factory by the whirr of machines and thud of the presser), businesslike, brisk and smart in his nice grey suit. A man of authority. In control. She felt a little shivery warmth that he was in control of her too. As he said, the silly girl was a passing phase. Here was a chance to get the boy back into the church choir. The minister, Reverend West, was constantly asking for him to join the new youth fellowship. Eileen thought Reverend West masculine and authoritative, but he was quite namby-pamby beside Lance. She dismissed forever a small and shameful dream of Mr West kissing her, his quirking mouth serious for the occasion. She had always been intrigued by the way his lips darted back, making a dent in his cheek before he actually parted them to smile. Behave yourself from now on, she told herself sternly, getting up her brightest smile to sneak open Allan's door. He was on his back reading a comic and slid his large, blotched face past the cover to stare at her.

"Your father said you're not to worry about a thing!" she said.

"That traitor!" Allan cried, and flinging the comic from him he swung over and buried his face in the pillow.

232

41

Although Kathleen had known Joe Miller for less than two weeks, it took a good part of the Saturday afternoon to explain his charms, real and imaginary, to Patricia.

Patricia, however, refused to be totally humbled in her role as the younger sister with the more menial job. There were gems to be offered from her first week as a wage earner and she was determined to offer them.

She had won praise from Mrs Campbell for her pyramid arrangement of display packets of tea, biscuits and dried fruits in the shop window, none of which were available yet from the shelves inside. Wartime restrictions had not been lifted, and Australia was exporting large quantities of goods to Britain, suffering more acutely the aftermath of war.

Daphne had not been a responsive audience when Patricia rushed home to tell her.

"Dud would have given his two eyes for a helpin' of rice custard! But where does all the damn rice go? Into the hollow innards of them Poms. We died for them in the war and now we starve for them in the peace!"

Patricia explained that the idea was to show customers what the shop would be selling when there was no more rationing, introducing the remark with "Mrs Campbell said", which had freely punctuated all her speech since she started her job.

"Just as well them two came from Scotland and not further down," Daphne said, scorning the use of the word England as she did its inhabitants. "Else you wouldn't be workin' for them, make no mistake about that!"

Patricia at this stage, unable to imagine an existence anywhere but behind Campbell's counter, vowed to keep from Daphne any hint of liaison with England or the English.

She jerked herself up now on her bed and wrapped her arms tightly around her knees, biting them in her agitation.

"If I meet a boy I like I'll have to ask him straight away if his grandmother comes from England.

"If she does I'll be sunk." She looked around the room, the first of her own, as if to assure herself it had not been swept away from her. Daphne had given her a chest of drawers from her own room and promised a cupboard John had made for brooms and dust pans, which could be spared from the side veranda and was seldom if ever used as John had intended.

"Madam has her eyes on it for her linen, but she's got another think comin'," Daphne had said. "We'll get it

234

cleaned up nice and in there with your dresses hangin' up before them weddin' bells start to peal."

Patricia's eyes rested on the corner where it would go and her mind dreamed up dresses she was most unlikely to own filling it.

"You know about the new wardrobe I'm getting?" Patricia addressed Kathleen's stomach, since her head was hanging over the side of the bed, her feet tapping the floor on one side and her hair sweeping it on the other.

"There will be times in my life," Kathleen said, "when I'll pine over Allan and what might have been."

Patricia did not ask what might have been but her silence did.

"A beautiful home, a life of leisure, tons of clothes, my own car, a maid probably." Her hair whooshed back and forth and her heels clicked together in time with her words.

"Do you know who is to blame for Allan and me?"

"Joe Miller!" Patricia cried with the certainty of being right.

The hair and the heels made a loud denial.

"It was over *centuries* before I even met Joe!

"No!" She swung herself around to face Patricia with her back to the end of the bed. Her eyes travelled over Patricia's face as if deciding whether she was able to bear the weight of the announcement to come.

"Sooner or later you will learn this. Madam Amy is preggers."

"What's that?"

Kathleen rolled her eyes towards the ceiling. Then she sketched a great hoop in the vicinity of her stomach.

Patricia's brown eyes flew very wide. "Dad?"

Kathleen collapsed on her stomach, head back over the edge of the bed. "You poor innocent!" she said to the underneath.

Patricia hauled her up by the shoulder and Kathleen clambered to the head of the bed, taking Patricia's pillow and stuffing a corner into her mouth. Her muffled laughter squeaked around it and her shaking body made the bed shake. Patricia was very still.

"Ted would be a mighty straight shot if he fired from the Moruya hotel to Crystal Street Petersham!" She rolled over on her back. "You convulse me!"

Patricia barely moved. She lowered her eyes and plucked at the quilt and when she finally looked up she was in tears. Kathleen plumped the pillow into its rightful place. "It's quite a serious matter," she said, head on the pillow, eyes on the ceiling. "But a laugh's as good as a tonic, you know."

In a moment Patricia got gently off the bed and began to brush her hair in front of the mirror with the tortoise-shell frame that had belonged to Daphne as a girl. She addressed her reflection. "I'm frightened."

Kathleen got up too and tidied her navy dress about the waist, unable to resist an affectionate little caressing of her flat stomach. Patricia saw in the mirror, and asked briefly with her eyes if Kathleen allowed boys to do more than kiss and cuddle her. She will tell me in time she thought, returning her thoughts to Amy.

"Poor Dad," she said. "I thought that he and Mum might—you know—"

Kathleen took the brush from Patricia and stroked her hair back from her forehead, wrinkling it, then wrinkling it more with worry that the lines might be permanent.

"Oh, I must stop frowning this way!" she said, addressing her own and Patricia's reflections in the mirror. Patricia was on the edge of the bed, her brown eyes very big in their wetness. Brown-eyed people look better crying than blue-eyed people, Kathleen thought, remembering Amy's weeping when she announced she was pregnant.

"Amy's been crying quite a bit," she said. "It's had that effect on her."

"Oh, poor Mum!" Patricia cried, taking up the pillow to dab her eyes.

Kathleen sat on the chair, now repaired by John at Daphne's insistence, the one propped against the wall when Amy had the room, and making her back very straight tapped the back of the brush thoughtfully on her knee. Patricia, now partly ashamed of her tears, thought how much she was like the teacher they all thought she would become.

"You wanted to be a teacher, didn't you?" she said.

Kathleen tossed the brush onto the chest and flung her legs out in a gesture of abandonment.

"Both Miss Parks and I broke our hearts when I had to leave."

"Aunty Daph said in her letters Mum wanted you to stay on."

Kathleen leapt to her feet and put her face close to the mirror to separate her eyelashes and pinch her eyebrows into an unruffled line, displaying a sudden and quite remarkable energy.

"My dear little Innocent! You can't take a scrap of notice of what people *say*. Amy may have talked a lot about me going on and becoming a teacher, etcetera and etcetera. But..." And she picked up her shoes to put them on, holding them up first to admire their slender line and high heel bought to impress both Joe Miller and Patricia, who was still in cuban heels from the general store in Moruya. "But...I must warn you that you have to live with people to discover what they are *really* like."

She took her handbag from the doorknob and swung it towards Patricia to indicate they were moving on.

"We'll go to Tina's. She has an older sister with fourteen children. Well, it *seems* she has that many. It's a good idea to keep reminding yourself how it *could be you.*

"I should have taken Amy there one Saturday arvo when Constance was visiting. Constant Constance, Tina and I call her.

"Would you believe, little sister, Amy actually seems to be *glad she is!*"

Amy did not face the real reason for putting off telling Lance until she recovered from the shock of telling him.

I think I knew all along what he would say. I just pretended to myself I wanted to enjoy the secret on my own. It was not that way at all.

She was walking around her bedroom in her petticoat, whispering to herself. She had taken off her yellow dress for relief from its tightness at her waist. She slithered the silk against her skin, taking pleasure from it in spite of the realization of being terribly alone.

She sat on the edge of her bed with her bare feet cooling on the linoleum (a gift from Lance) thinking she did not hate him, or even resent him, wondering why this was so. She licked a tear running into the corner of her mouth, not knowing about it until she tasted the salt. Perhaps I *am* a little mad, she thought.

She hadn't intended telling Lance the way she did. After work one Thursday, he took her to a cafe opposite Railway Square for the asparagus on toast she loved. Allan was not with him.

"I've left him to get the tram home," Lance explained, moving the salt and pepper to get a better view of Amy's face. A purple shade of lipstick was fashionable that year. It darkened Amy's blue eyes to violet. Lance liked it.

"He needs to get some independence," Lance said, leaving the violet for a moment. "You can make 'em too soft."

Amy's face went soft. She saw a little boy with serious brown eyes and a sturdy body struggling up steps, refusing to hang onto a rail, brushing her hands aside.

Lance usually avoided mention of Allan or Kathleen. Amy was glad of this. It helped reinforce her dream of the coming child as the real son of Lance. She fancied a future of Eileen and Allan together, more like wife and husband than mother and son, and herself, Lance and the baby in a separate household. Perhaps the Petersham house, Amy would think, looking around it and making mental changes to accommodate Lance.

Had Lance known, he might have envied Amy the luxury of fantasy. Or fantasy of a nature distinct from his. He worried that Allan, since his rejection by Kathleen, might tell Eileen of the affair with Amy in a fit of spite. His mental picture of the ensuing scene would send him running to Allan's side to check out his mood.

On one occasion Allan left a five-pound note on the counter after serving a customer with dry cleaning, then went and bowed his head in despondency over the ironing board, oblivious to the light patter of feet when the next customer saw the money and made a run for it, taking his overcoat to the rival cleaners and the cash to the Prince of Wales on the next corner.

All Lance could allow himself for relief was a hard slamming of the till and a rush for the factory with barely a glimpse of Allan's tragic, guilty face.

There Lance's own guilt took over. The boy was the only thing that was really his! He couldn't risk losing him! He might leave Lincolns and go into a bank (Eileen fancied banks and sighed over the neat young men in them), and leave the way open for Tom's son. He rushed back to the dry cleaning shop to tell Allan he would relieve him, and Allan could give Victor a hand in the office with some practice on the adding machine, something he knew made Allan feel superior.

Amy told Lance she was pregnant after they had left the cafe and had passed Grace Brothers' windows. They stopped to look at a georgette dress the colour of Amy's lipstick, displayed on a wax model.

The top bloused over a tight waist, and the skirt was narrow and knife pleated. The collar was a soft scarf with a tiny pearl button holding it in place.

Lance wanted her to have it.

"I know you sew your own things," he said, gripping her hand hard in case her feelings might be hurt. "But just for a change why don't you have that dress?"

She loved him for not saying he would pay for it, though she knew he would.

"Let's sit for a while on the church seat," she said.

The seat faced Broadway, and the traffic fed into George Street at two intersections. Amy noticed a car, a navy blue Chevrolet filled with young people in fancy dress, obviously on their way to a party. The men were in straw boaters and striped blazers, and the girls were very blonde or very dark with heads coming from layered collars. Like painted gumnuts with leaves still on the twig, Amy thought.

Lance cried out: "Why didn't you say something sooner?" His face was so ugly she had to turn quickly from it, mainly in fear that she would remember it only that way.

She had held his hand tightly, partly to ascertain through the feel of his flesh if he loved her still.

She let the hand go. And pulled her skirt down, for it had a habit of riding up, and Amy thought his face flinched watching her. Perhaps she merely felt the flinch, because his eyes appeared to be on the traffic. She wondered if he was not really seeing it, although he appeared to be, and thought how silly and naive she was to have believed all this time that she always knew what he was thinking.

A bank of trees struggling for a show of greenness against the dust separated the church from the pavement. Amy saw a small bird land on a twig not strong enough to hold it. The bird flung its little cocked-up tail around and with a triumphant tweet hopped to a stronger branch and slid its beak along a leaf, gobbling at the moisture with an eager throat and rapidly blinking eyes.

Amy got up and walked quickly to the pavement and crossed the street to the tram stop. She was grateful that the traffic came on heavier, shutting out Lance's figure should he be following. She did not look back even from the safety of the tram.

I think I'll go home to have the baby, she said to herself, keeping the picture of the little bird in her mind.

Lance sent her a letter.

Dear Amy (it said), I'm sorry. Telephone me here at the factory. Lance.

In other notes he had said Dearest Amy and put Love at the bottom. She began to crumple the page then smoothed it out and decided to put it with the others from him, including the first he had written, asking her to dinner to celebrate her ownership of the furniture. She had a chocolate box partly filled and when she closed the lid she was terribly sad that the envelopes would be jostled about in there with no support from each other, no chance for them now to be tightly packed as she once thought, perhaps with the need for a larger box.

She wondered if she should throw them out and use the box for something else, perhaps a crochet hook and some cotton with which she would work on some table mats or a collar and cuffs set, or something for the baby while she was in hospital. Lying on her bed again in her petticoat she decided to dismiss the idea of table mats since she would soon have no place of her own.

Immediately she got home from work she took off her dress, the buttons fastening it in front now transferred to the extreme edge, and got the evening meal in her petticoat. It was December and very hot weather, and the first week after she told Lance about the baby.

Kathleen changed into shorts and a cotton knit top Amy got cheaply from Lincolns because the machinist had put a pale blue cuff on one sleeve and a darker shade on the other. Amy had unpicked the sleeves, cut strips from them and bound the armholes. She wore it for two summers, then Kathleen said it was no use to Amy while she was "like that" and took it for herself.

Kathleen looked with distaste at Amy peeling potatoes with the straps of her petticoat slipping from her shoulders and some strands of hair dangling towards her nose.

"One day the Misses Sweetleys will see you like that and all will be revealed," Kathleen said.

"Shut up and set the table."

"God, that counter at A.H.'s isn't going to hide you forever, Amy."

Amy sat to slice the handful of beans she had gathered from the garden. She smiled on them. They were such a tender green, supple but not limp, a delicate little spring curling from their tops. It seemed a shame to have to tear it away.

"At least you've stopped weeping," Kathleen said.

Amy got up to find a saucepan. Her petticoat was stuck to the points of her buttocks, and the backs of her knees were exposed like pale pink blotting paper marked with a blue pencil.

"How can I ask Joe to tea with you looking like that?"

"If you do, warn him there's worse to come."

"You disgust me. Not just the way you are either."

Amy sent a rush of water over the beans.

"Have you heard from Grease Pot?" Kathleen asked.

"No. Have you heard from the Junior Size?"

"No," said Kathleen. "Nor do I want to."

Amy was at the stove and a lot of her neck showed above the petticoat. Bent with the hair parted it looked as young as Lebby's as Kathleen remembered her.

"Amy!" she cried and Amy turned with the saucepan poised above the flaring jet, her eyes like the blue flame yet to gather warmth.

Kathleen got up and flung a cloth on the table. I nearly said I'd help you, Amy, she said to herself, biting her lip in confusion.

She turned her back to show Amy her own bowed neck and took cutlery from the kitchen drawer.

44

Kathleen suggested Patricia come into Anthony Horderns and meet Joe Miller.

"You can give me the lowdown on what you think," Kathleen said.

"But are you going to marry him?" Patricia saw herself as bridesmaid.

"Depends," Kathleen said.

Patricia wanted to say "On what?" but felt the inadequacy of one who believed the luxury of such a choice would always evade her.

They were in blouses and shorts over bathing suits on the back steps of the Petersham house. Patricia had stayed overnight and slept on the lounge. Amy had never allowed the lounge to be used this way before. Now she did not care. She felt it had betrayed her, as Lance had.

It being Sunday, Kathleen and Patricia were going to Bondi.

"Where it all began," Kathleen whispered to Patricia, rolling her eyes towards the kitchen window, behind which Amy was washing the breakfast things.

They were delayed in getting away. The front gate clicked open, and they both jumped up and ran to meet Daphne with tear marks on her face and a screwed-up handkerchief in her hand.

"Aunty Daph!" Patricia cried.

Daphne gave her head a little shake and went faster into the house to meet Amy coming out.

"Aunty Daph!" Amy echoed.

Under her breath Kathleen said: "Hell, what now?"

"It's come to an 'ead," Daphne said, unclicking her handbag to put her wet handkerchief there.

Amy took her elbow and steered her into the lounge room. She sat and occupied herself for a moment with spreading a fresh handkerchief on the arm of her chair.

"I should get covers,' Amy murmured, briefly back on good terms with the lounge.

"Although I suppose it's a little late now."

"It makes two of us," Daphne said.

Patricia turned a little pale and looked around the room as if it might be swept away at any moment and she should memorize it. Kathleen leaned back in the corner of her chair and made her face quiet.

"You'd know without me tellin' what Madam wants," Daphne said.

"Your house," Kathleen said.

Patricia jumped with a wild look around the room as if this time it was really going. Then she put an arm around Daphne's neck and laid a cheek on her shoulder.

Amy watched as she closed her eyes, channelling the full force of her love to Daphne.

Amy raised her legs and laid them crossways on her chair, nudging the bulge of her stomach gently with her knee. He's safe there, she thought. All mine. Loving no other than me.

She sent a small frowning glance to Kathleen and Patricia.

"There's nothing stopping you two going off to the beach."

"Whatever is going to happen to us?" Patricia whispered to Kathleen. They were in the tram, which was shrieking as it turned its nose up Oxford Street on its way to the coast.

They passed mean little balconies with people lined up on them watching with dreams in their eyes. Patricia was surprised to see an absence of envy and discontent in their expressions, since there appeared to be no prospect of their going to the beach.

They were crossing the sand looking for a place to leave their towels when Kathleen paused, rushed on and hissed: "Look neither to left or right, but straight ahead! Fix your eyes on that buoy four breakers out and do not move them!"

Patricia immediately looked to either side and behind her, stumbling over a pair of legs belonging to a sunbather and pitching forward to arouse the attention of every group within a radius of fifty yards.

Kathleen ran so fast then, jumping over bodies and sending sand flying into faces that Patricia, scrambling to her feet, was afraid she would lose her. Kathleen dropped down at last near a Greek family, the women in black headscarves and the men in navy serge trousers and sandshoes, all solid enough to make a protective wall, and there she lay getting her breath back in little moaning pants.

"Oh, look what you've gone and done!" She closed her eyes and pushed her face into the sand as if she were planning on suffocation. Patricia put a hesitant hand between her shoulder blades. She withdrew it from the quivering flesh, and on her knees peered over the heads of the Greek people for clues among the crowd. Kathleen sat up and pressed her face between her knees.

"He's here," she said.

"Joe?"

"No other." Kathleen squeezed her eyes shut.

"Now I don't have to ask Mrs Campbell can I go early on Friday night for a gander!"

"You certainly don't." Kathleen stood and turned her back in the direction of Joe.

"I'd like a look," Patricia said with a trace of wistfulness.

"Go ahead while I take a swim." Kathleen began easing her shorts down over her hips, bringing sparks to the eyes of the Greek men. "Look out for a lump of lard, but make haste before it melts and there's nothing left but a straw hat." She folded her shorts with great care, no tremor in her long fine hands among the folds. "He's wearing, I'll have you know, his school hat! To let everyone know he went to a posh school. Not a trace of a suntan.

250

"I'd be humiliated beyond words to set foot on a beach without a suntan!"

"Was he all by himself?" Patricia asked, not entirely innocent.

Kathleen ran fast towards the water and Patricia following did not see her face.

"He may have been, or he may not have been!" Kathleen leapt over small waves poised for breaking. "As far as I'm concerned he's by himself from now on!"

They were leaving the beach, going up the steps to the boulevard when Kathleen gripped Patricia, who winced at the hurt to her sunburned arm.

"I was descending these steps when I first saw Allan Yates," she said. "This place is doomed for me. Let's leave it behind forever!"

She raced for the tram stop with Patricia, who was growing a little plump through eating too many broken biscuits at Campbells, a few paces behind.

When they flopped down on the seat for waiting passengers, Kathleen took out her compact and fastidiously flicked sand from little crevices in her face and among her eyebrows. She continued her toilet, combing her hair and rolling the ends under, until the tram rumbled towards them.

"I might write to Allan Yates tonight," she said, swinging her bag onto her arm. "Never a weekend passed that he didn't take me somewhere.

"We never passed a cafe that he didn't drag me into for coffee and cake, magnificent toasted sandwiches.

Nothing was too good for me. To hell with Amy and her wanton ways!"

They climbed on the tram and needing to strap-hang, Kathleen had to continue in a mutter, her lips crushed against her raised arm.

"I'll write and bring him running!"

45

But she wrote to Miss Parks instead.

It was quite late in the evening before she shut her bedroom door. Daphne was still at the house when she and Patricia got back, still in the lounge room with Amy.

Patricia rushed straight in to take Daphne's hand and sit close to her. It was plain that Daphne had shed a great many tears during their absence. The handkerchief she had spread on the chair arm was now crumpled on her lap, and her leathery skin was blotched with a pale beetroot colour, darker on the tip of her nose. Amy had given her a face washer wrung out in cold water to dab on her forehead. The washer was laid across a shoulder and Patricia jumped and had to stifle a giggle when her cheek felt the unexpected chill.

Amy's face had taken on its customary late-Sunday expression of anxiety, contrasting with the relief when she turned her back on curious and suspicious eyes leaving work at midday on Saturday. Now her eyes and mouth betrayed the torment of facing them again on Monday morning.

But she told herself she must worry more for Daphne. Dudley had died without leaving life insurance, the house was not fully paid for and Peter's gratuity pay for war service was almost gone.

She would need to go out to work and after twenty-five years, she doubted that she would find work at her old trade of seamstress.

"I would find it easier to bear but for the way she put it," Daphne moaned. "'He'll get the place eventually.'"

Amy made sympathetic noises with tongue and teeth.

Daphne rubbed her eyes briefly with the washer, and forgetting it wasn't a handkerchief squeezed it in her hand, causing a little trickle of moisture onto Patricia's arm and another stifled giggle.

"I wish I was lyin' beside Dud, except that's exactly what she wants!"

I am alive and giving life, Amy thought. It's not wrong that I feel glad.

"Everything goes against you," Daphne moaned on. "I lose Peter then Dud, and all I have left gets into the clutches of that crowd. Dud never took to them." She laid the washer back on her shoulder.

"I don't suppose now the way things have gone with you and the Yates man there's any chance of me gettin' work in his factory.

"My eyes are not that good for fine work, but I can still make good buttonholes. I was always the best at buttonholes."

Amy made more soothing noises, this time with wistful overtones.

She had to fight off a swift vision of Lance at the finishers' table watching the women, chin resting on the sharp ridge of his collar, two fingers in a waistcoat pocket. Then if he saw her his chin would jerk sharply up, his body moving involuntarily, as if he would skirt the table to reach her, but instead taking himself in control, looking back on the women's work with a deepening frown, furrowing their brows too and setting up a new nervousness in their fingers.

"Your buttonholes are always perfect," Amy murmured.

"To think of the hundreds I made for them! Never a dress or skirt that didn't come over the fence for me to finish off!"

"Don't think about it," Amy pleaded.

"She won't be callin' on me for the weddin' dress. Make no mistake there!"

There was the sound of Kathleen and Patricia beating their young feet on the steps coming in.

Amy got off the chair arm. "It's time for us to refill that teapot," she said.

"I should be goin' 'ome," Daphne said piteously.

"'Ome! I wonder how long I'll be callin' it that!"

Kathleen wrote to Miss Parks:

I have intended writing for a long time but it is not until now that I have *completely* made up my mind.

I am going to get more education. I have had some disastrous experiences with *men*. I absolutely loathe them. I want to become something, at this stage I'm not sure what, but you are the one person who can advise me. I know I must first get my Leaving Certificate and this should be possible by going to night school, which I am prepared to do.

As you know I broke my heart at leaving when I did, but such were the circumstances. Apart from my attitude towards men and my decision to blot them out of my life forever, I am disappointed in my mother, Amy. You would have witnessed the diabolical behaviour of mothers in your time and I can add one more sample to them. I have suffered greatly through her. First she left me at the tender age of four, and then brought great turmoil and embarrassment to my life by pretending we were sisters in order to act years younger than her rightful age and pretend to the world at large that she was without responsibilities. As you know, it was to relieve her of the burden of keeping me at school that I left to go into my present dead-end job. The only compensation is the books I can read during the dull, so deadly dull times. Even this is fraught with problems since the floorwalker wants a duster in my hand when I'm not wrapping books or ringing up the till. I am absolutely green with envy when people (students, groan, groan) come in to buy Shakespeare, Homer, T. S. Eliot and the like. Those are the only men in my life from now on.

But you would rap me over the knuckles at the way I have changed course (as you used to say) without an eye to correct *structure*. I beg your tolerance, and will forthwith return to the point. After surviving the era of Amy-my-sister-and-not-my-mother I am now faced with the coming of an illegitimate child to the same person. Yes! This and some quite devastating personal experiences have turned me off men, motherhood and everything connected with it. I want to get an education, follow a career, travel and be happy in the companionship of someone with whom I'm intellectually matched. And that, dear Miss Parks, is someone of your *ilk*.

257

Write to me here if you care to, but make haste if that is not asking too much, for there is another trauma in my life with Amy at the helm as you would expect, and that is we must leave here soon. She will soon be dismissed from her job and I cannot be expected to meet the rent and provide for myself and my sister as well. Then again, my younger sister was recklessly brought to Sydney and has this dreadful job behind a grocer's counter. Could you imagine such a life? There is another sister still to come. Our Amy is quite prolific as you can see.

Oh Miss Parks I need to be rescued. Most desperately I need to be *rescued*.

Your former (and loving) pupil,
Kathleen Fowler.

In the days that followed Kathleen relieved the boredom of work by repeating under her breath some of the best lines from her letter.

"You have witnessed the diabolical behaviour of mothers," she whispered, taking a copy of *Tom Brown's Schooldays* from a shelf and putting it between the shabby gloves of a woman who looked a lot like one of the Misses Wheatley. The gloves stroked it as if it were some rare first edition.

"A Christmas present for my grandson," she said, bringing her watery glasses to life with the shine in her watery eyes.

She's been a mother then, thought Kathleen. What a fool. She swept a fine white hand over the brown paper she wrapped the book in, keeping her eyes on it, not changing her expression when Mr Benson padded up to express a wish that the customer would enjoy the book, and to compliment her on her wisdom in shopping at Anthony Horderns. Kathleen turned her back immediately to find another copy of *Tom Brown's Schooldays* to fill the gap, and Mr Benson, glaring at her back, decided that the Fowler women had failed to be the acquisition to Anthony Horderns he had once thought. Mrs Fowler would need to go as soon as the Christmas rush was over. He had got Mrs Benson to come in and confirm what was now common gossip on the floor. Easily four months, Mrs Benson had said, and he shut himself in the floor manager's office to share with him this scandalous revelation. But he was told coldly the matter was in hand, for the manager's wife was an embittered, harping, barren woman and the manager indulged in fantasies while he sneaked his eyes over Amy's changing figure, dreaming of sleeping beside her, his dry thin hand on her stomach, sliding down to the crevice where her thigh joined it, exploring there, the leap of his blood with hers when she turned and flung her leg across his.

Oh my God, he said to the blurred page in his open Daily Staff Record Book.

Amy saw Mr Benson leave Kathleen's counter and come towards hers, and to avoid him, bent down to straighten bolts of material, already in pin-neat order. She heard a button on her navy dress pop off and saw the gap, open-mouthed with relief.

259

That does it, she said to herself, I'll go and see
Mr Henty at once. Whatever he says to me I'll just have to
bear it, and say nothing in return.

But he said: "Sit down, Mrs Fowler.

"You're on your feet too much."

Daphne planned to move with Patricia into the Petersham house in time for Christmas.

The Misses Wheatley planned to have moved out by then.

Amy's pregnancy decided them.

"See, Grace," said Miss Heather, opening one of the dear little drawers that ran like silk in a circular cedar table.

She took out the cutting of Amy's advertisement seeking tenants for her rooms, the old maroon-coloured fingers plucking it from among Christmas cards from Henry, the obituaries in the Dubbo paper recording the deaths of their parents, and a recipe for a Dundee cake which they had not made for twenty years.

"'Rooms in clean, respectable house'," Miss Heather read aloud in a voice mingling emotion with disgust.

"'Share conveniences with single lady.' Poor Mumma would turn in her grave."

"Poor Papa would turn with her," Miss Grace said.

They were getting ready to go and see Mrs Murray, the wife of the minister at the church they attended. Mrs Murray, who had been the matron's assistant at a church boarding school before her marriage, made herself available for counselling in crises other than those of a spiritual nature.

The Misses Wheatley were intending to explain their circumstances as delicately as possible.

"We are lucky to have Mrs Murray," Miss Heather said. "You couldn't very well approach a man."

"Mrs Murray will most likely know of somewhere for us," Miss Grace said.

"God is so good to us," said Miss Heather, putting on her round little shiny straw hat, getting a fresh thrill at the success she had made of turning the ribbon band to the other side, and folding the bow in such a way that only the best parts showed.

On the stairs they nearly turned back. Daphne and Amy were surveying the length of the hall, Daphne trying to decide if her hall runner would be long enough and annoyed that she hadn't measured it before leaving home.

Miss Heather's back told Miss Grace they might turn back. But the pause lasted hardly a second. We are not the guilty party, said Miss Heather's navy blue crepe shoulders and the rush of air up her nostrils. They continued on determined feet and were soon looking down into Daphne's upturned face, a pleased and amiable one.

"Just the two I wanted to see!" Daphne said. "You'll be payin' the rent to me from now on. I'm movin' in and we'll get on fine."

The Misses Wheatley for the first time in weeks managed to keep their eyes from Amy's stomach. They held the bannisters in their gnarled, gloved hands and Daphne's bold brown eyes with theirs.

"I'll come up," Daphne said with an upward movement of her arms as if she were urging two sheep up a ramp.

"My, you have it nice," Daphne said, looking around the Misses Wheatleys' sitting room, thereby giving herself leave to stroke a rose-splashed china fruit bowl containing a single orange.

"We were going out for the messages," Miss Heather said, daring Miss Grace with a frown to contradict her.

"Then I won't keep you," Daphne said, moving to the edge of a round-bottomed tapestry-covered chair with arms like melting milk chocolate.

"One little thing," said Daphne with earnest eyes on the Misses Wheatleys' glasses. "I'll be puttin' a little notice in the front window of the downstairs sittin' room where Mrs Fowler—"

"We never got used to saying Mrs Fowler—" murmured Miss Grace.

"Then you don't need to try any more," Daphne said. "Because Mrs Fowler's goin' back to her 'ome town—"

The Misses Wheatleys' glasses were like a collision of wheels sending out shrieks and sparks as metal hit metal.

"I'm going to do 'ome dressmaking," Daphne explained. "I'll do most of the work in the daytime, so's the machine won't bother you at night."

"We never hear a sound once we're in bed," Miss Heather said. And mindful suddenly of not hearing what might have been worth straining their ears for, she blushed and the pearl brooch shaped like a lily trembled on the crepe.

"My son John, the only one left, is takin' over my 'ouse." Daphne decided to get it all said now and if she chose to, restrict future communication with the Misses Wheatley to a bidding of the time of day.

"It's too out of the way for me to 'ave me business there," Daphne said, allowing a recurring dream to invade her thoughts—of someone's silk dress whispering against the wood of her machine and Patricia's brown head bowed over someone else's dress, while her hands made a neat job of turning up a raw hem. I don't see why not, she said to herself, getting up with energy and assuming a severe expression to impress on the Misses Wheatley the association of landlady and tenant and nothing more.

When Daphne had gone the Misses Wheatley took off their hats and put them away on the top shelf of their handsome rosewood wardrobe. They sat on their chairs on either side of the window overlooking Crystal Street. There was nothing unusual to see, only the baker's cart drawn by a brown horse with a woolly coat and a knotted mane, throwing its head wearily at the flies and moving the cart against the wishes of the delivery man, who called out "Woa!" and went around the front with his basket, clouting the side of the horse's head as he passed.

The Misses Wheatley usually winced at such a sight and thought of the beautiful proud animals at home on the farm, but looking at each other now, they each gave a gentle shake of their grey heads.

"I can only think of God's great goodness to us," Miss Heather said.

"So can I," said Miss Grace.

On the Saturday before Amy left for Diggers Creek, Kathleen told her she was going to live with Miss Parks.

"But I bought you a single bed!" Amy cried.

Kathleen went on as if Amy hadn't spoken. "Miss Parks has a huge flat with a huge bedroom and a bed big enough for both of us.

"Put my old bed under your arm and take it as a present for Lebby. She was sleeping on the couch the last I heard!"

They were eating a lunch of bread and cheese at Amy's bare kitchen table. The tablecloths had been packed with her other linen and her kitchenware to go by rail to Nowra then by lorry to Moruya. Daphne had lent them a couple of saucepans and some crockery for the last few meals before Amy and her suitcase boarded the train at Central. Daphne urged Amy to take most of her household goods.

"May'll appreciate some new things. She wouldn't have had much for herself for a long time."

No she wouldn't, Amy thought, startled by her guilt, and Daphne said quickly: "It'll seem more like 'ome to me if I have all me own things around me."

She grumbled about Amy giving the lounge suite to John. "He did so many little things about the place for me," Amy pleaded.

"I hate the thought of that great arse of hers squashin' the life out of it," Daphne said. Amy gave the cane dressing-table to an ecstatic Patricia.

Just when it seemed there was some sort of future for them all, here was this new blow delivered by Kathleen.

"I'll take my desk!" she said. "Miss Parks has made me a space for it." She had cleaned it out and rubbed it down with furniture polish, clicking her tongue at some freshly revealed scratches she made herself, but blamed on Amy. She polished the brass corner pieces, her deep frown suggesting that this should have been done regularly but had been carelessly overlooked (by Amy).

Amy had to make a visit to Annandale to inform Daphne of the new development.

"Good riddance to her Ladyship!" Daphne cried, using tissue paper lavishly to wrap her best cutlery and store it in a shoebox.

She had just come from the side veranda and had glimpsed Mrs Cousins, with whom she was no longer on speaking terms, watching through the latticed end of her back veranda.

Daphne had the presence of mind to shout out: "I measured up and all the curtains will fit the new windows!" which brought a curious Patricia from her bedroom and sent Mrs Cousins, with a face as red as the hibiscus she believed was concealing her, scuttling inside.

"I just fixed next door!" Daphne said, turning a kitchen chair on one leg from the table for Amy to sit down. "I'll make a bed for the cat out of me curtains before I'll leave them for her!"

"I'm worried," Amy said, "that you might have been depending on some board money from Kathleen."

"What you'd get from her she'd take back via the iron and the lights and the gas on sky high and butter spread inches thick on her bread.

"Trish can have a room to herself and her Ladyship's bed will come in handy if we can ever afford to bring Lebby up for a holiday. If my sewin' goes well we'll be doing that!"

But Lebby's mind was on matters other than Sydney and her relatives there.

She was going to become a boarder at Moruya convent and study under the nuns for her Intermediate Certificate.

For the past few months Lebby had joined a small class of girls taken by Sister Louise. She called it a business course with elementary instruction in bookkeeping (for she could keep only one lesson ahead of her pupils), and shorthand and typing, at which she was more proficient.

The class was looking towards work with banks, solicitors or grain merchants in Moruya, or perhaps Nowra or Bega.

But Sister Louise, with an ear for their chatter between lessons and an eye for their shortened skirts and stealthily painted lips and nails, shrewdly assumed the more prominent target was a husband.

Lesley Fowler was different.

One afternoon in the convent music room, where she could watch for the approach of the mail car to take her home to Diggers Creek, she picked up a violin, and putting it under her creamy chin, drew sounds from it that were nothing like a cat's wailing, and far superior to those made by the Potter sisters and Desmond O'Reilly, who had been learning for two years.

Sisters Louise and Anastasia, of the same mind, agreed to go and see May.

They praised Lebby's learning ability, her obvious appreciation of the arts, her ladylike manner and nice speaking voice, and said she would waste her life in an office. They looked carefully down May's hall over the wild front garden to the roadway, lest their eyes give away their hopes that Lebby be spared a future spent trying to keep ordered a dirty little house like this and a brood of dirty children.

The nuns left and Gus came in and took Lebby on his knee on the rocker, and May, impressed by the whiteness of the nuns' wimples and the high polish on their shoes, felt the need to clean the kitchen as a belated mark of respect, and to help eradicate her shame that they had witnessed her housekeeping at its worst.

She swept the small deal table under the window clear of its cut pumpkin, dripping tin, flour, sugar and tea bins and scrubbed it clean, her hands like two restless row boats in a foamy grey sea.

Gus lifted the curls from the back of Lebby's neck and blew on her skin as he had done since she was a few months old.

"It'll cost me that paddock of steers and the old sow and her next litter," Gus said, giving Lebby's neck a few little bites, causing her to giggle and shriek as she had done since she was one.

The presence of the nuns still invaded the kitchen, infecting May with the disturbing thought that they were able to witness the spectacle of Gus and Lebby.

She sent the bins and pumpkin skittering back onto the damp table.

"Now cut that out! She's gettin' a bit big for that caper!"

Lebby stood with a serious face and smoothed her dress down to sit sedately on the sofa. Gus got up to look for his tobacco on the shelf.

"They'll not be askin' for the full fee by the way they were talkin'," May said to make amends for the reprimand and bring joy back to Lebby's face.

"So long as they don't get her into a black hood and on her knees from mornin' till night."

"Oh Pa!" Lebby laughed with a big shake of her head.

Amy did not like Lebby. She was irritated by her giggle and the way she clung onto Gus, rushing to him when he came inside and walking in the paddocks pressed to his side.

She did little or no work in the house, and May appeared to overlook this while constantly complaining of the chaos.

Amy had dreaded a meeting with Ted, but he was gone by the time she got to Diggers Creek.

"I might as well tell you right off he's shot through again," May said brutally, then repented at Amy's rush of tears, mistakenly believing Amy had been depending on Ted's support.

Amy picked up her case and took it to the room she would share with Lebby until Lebby left for the convent in a few weeks' time.

"I will be by myself, thank goodness," she whispered to the mantlepiece where she would put her treasured vases and china cats.

She marked out a space with her eyes where she would put a cot, the iron one she had slept in herself, roped to the rafters of the shed. She would paint it white and hang it with mosquito net.

I mean I'll be by myself only until he comes, she corrected her thoughts, feeling the need to apologize. She thought of waking early and watching for him to wake and snuffle and move his hard little head, butting at the pillow.

I wonder who he will look like, she thought. Me, perhaps. I hope.

She did not see Lance again, although she nearly chanced to. He had a new car which she did not recognize when he passed the house on his way down the south coast taking Eileen and Allan and Allan's new girlfriend Marjorie.

Lance thought from Amy's description of the Scriveners' place it was somewhere hereabouts. But instead of slowing down to try and pick it out, he pressed the

271

accelerator and shot ahead, in sudden fear that Allan, given a similar description by Kathleen, might become suspicious.

But Allan was totally engrossed in Marjorie, an arm along the back of the seat holding her shoulder, his other hand holding hers in her lap.

Marjorie's free hand was arranging and rearranging her hat, a green one with flying yellow ribbons, and the bobbing green and yellow hat was all that Amy saw, lifting her eyes briefly from her baby son sleeping on her knee.

The car made her remember, though, sitting on the veranda long ago with the other children, dreaming of being carried away to a better life.

She did not have those children any more.

Miss Parks had Kathleen, Daphne had Patricia, and May and Gus or perhaps the nuns at St Margaret's had Lebby.

But this one was hers to keep forever. She crushed him so hard against her he squirmed and whimpered, and she had to rock him quiet again.

Text Classics

textclassics.com.au